AS THEY WERE

As They Were

M. J. MOBLEY

RESOURCE *Publications* · Eugene, Oregon

AS THEY WERE

Resource Publications
An Imprint of Wipf and Stock Publishers
199 W. 8th Ave., Suite 3
Eugene, OR 97401

www.wipfandstock.com

PAPERBACK ISBN: 978-1-6667-3707-3
HARDCOVER ISBN: 978-1-6667-9616-2
EBOOK ISBN: 978-1-6667-9617-9

04/06/22

This is a work of fiction. Any references to historical events, real people, or real places are used fictitiously. Names, characters, and places are products of the author's imagination.

The eight-line poem extract contained herein is from "Alastor; or, The Spirit of Solitude," by Percey Bysshe Shelley, first UK publication 1816. Public domain.

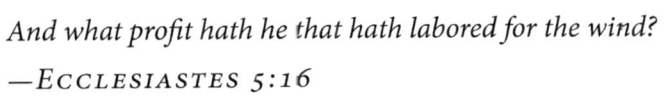

And what profit hath he that hath labored for the wind?
—ECCLESIASTES 5:16

1.

CALL ME OBEDIENT TO a higher calling. Call me a fool. Whatever you call me, here I am, until you move on and I am no longer called anything.

I have come to believe I was drawn to this place by my own adventur-ous constitution, by a need to feel something deeper in the world, by a desire to ward off the deep sense of angst buried deep within my conscious. Nev-ertheless, that one fateful day a village elder handed me an unripe pear and accused my soldiers of malfeasance caught me off guard. Maybe I should have been better prepared. But it is difficult to see the entire truth while still in the moment, like trying to patch holes in the hull of a sinking ship, the water slowly enveloping you until, before the truth of your situation becomes evident, your fate is forever sealed in the watery belly of the beast.

The command of Combat Outpost Chemera, a small, company-sized, mud-wall-and-sandbag fortress five kilometers from an international bor-der dividing two worlds—one at war with an insurgency and one pretend-ing to not be supporting that insurgency—falls to me. I am responsible for everything that does and does not happen on Chemera. This is my job. And a commander has no time for discussion, quibbling, or arguing regarding his implementation as a soldier. We have no say in the matter. In the end, the myriad ways in which my existence plays out in Combat Outpost Chem-era should be of little concern to me. Besides, which side you support and whose side of this story you believe depends on which side of any number of borders you fall.

The events both before and after my interaction with the pear-wielding elder that day are filtered, of course. But all stories are refined in one way or another before they reach you, are they not? My story, such as it is, happens to be filtered and purified through the shimmering haze of a smoldering trash pit much wider than it needs to be and not nearly deep enough to serve its purpose. You know this burn pit, dear reader, if it is the only thing you know of this conflict. To understand this narrative filtration is the first step in understanding my story.

So you may call me whatever you like. Because here I am, right now, present for duty, as I swore to be in the very beginning of my creation as a soldier. This is my chosen profession, my calling, if you will, a calling for which I am removed from my home and employed in the defense of our nation to be tucked away in the rugged, high-desert foothills of mountain ranges the names of which we will never bother to learn, sent to exact revenge and to ensure our nation's foreign policy objectives are carried out in accordance with military rules and regulations.

There is in fact disagreement in our own nation as to what this insurgency is and who it is we are fighting, just as there is disagreement and confusion within the country we invaded, disagreement and confusion within the insurgency, and disagreement and confusion across the border. The only place where disagreement does not seem to exist arrives in the large care packages sent by the well-meaning, patriotic citizens of our homeland, care packages that are quickly rifled through for any food and snacks that have not already melted and are then discarded to the burn pit, the well-meaning and loving cards of encouragement along with cotton tube-socks, cheap razors, and paperback books tossed into the steaming stew of detritus and human waste smoldering just outside the mud walls of Combat Outpost Chemera. These boxes are complete. And they are wholesome. They represent all that is good in our nation, a people turning a blind eye—maybe consciously, maybe unconsciously—to the truth of our mission. But the tired, battle-worn realists who receive these packages only desire the contents that might provide shallow, superficial, and transitory comfort. The remainder, with hardly a second thought, is tossed away.

There are several small villages in my assigned area of operations, an area that covers nearly fifty square kilometers. Most of these villages consist of three or four extended families, hidden and tucked away in mountains and valleys and high desert wadis. These people are undisturbed, pure, unchanged and unconquered. A few villages are, of course, larger, but not so big as to constitute more than what would be a one-stoplight town in our own nation. The closest village to me and the men living out their present lives at Combat Outpost Chemera is the village of Gaumela, which lies directly on an international border. At least, Gaumela is depicted as being situated on top of the border on the maps we have been provided and which serve as the guide for patrolling and navigating my assigned area of operations. No one is quite sure which country takes ownership of the village of Gaumela, a testament to the tenuous hold these two countries hold to any semblance of real governance. Or physical maps. Or borders.

The citizens of Gaumela do not care about their geographic location on an international border. Most may not even be fully aware that they straddle a recognized political boundary. These citizens only care about the mystical time-defying present that is Gaumela. And where to next graze their goat herds. I would not care about Gaumela's location myself were it not for the fact that both my superiors and I believe that Gaumela serves as a safe haven for insurgents and as a thoroughfare for the transport of weapons and bombs from one side of the border across to the other side of the border and further into the country we currently occupy in hopes of utilizing this smuggled ordinance to inflict death and destruction upon our nation's army. We further believe Gaumela to be the source of numerous rockets those of us assigned to Chemera absorb on a regular basis. The enemies of my country, the insurgents, if you will, use this international border to their advantage by hopping across the border, firing their rockets at Chemera, and then running back across to the safety afforded them by the neighboring country.

I do not question the efficacy of their tactics. I would utilize these tactics myself were I to find myself involved in an insurgency after an invasion and if the invading army failed to secure the border or otherwise failed to account for the disposition of neighboring countries before they embarked on their invasion and occupation. The citizens of Gaumela are right not to take sides. They are stuck in the middle, whether they realize it or not, pawns in a power struggle between our nation and our declared enemy.

Our nation's foreign policy would best be served if the citizens of Gaumela were to rise up against the enemy and prevent these insurgents from acting with impunity within the country we have invaded and occupied. But sometimes grazing your goats and growing food for your family is more important than making a decision on what form of government to accept in your life, even when an obviously superior conquering army offers you a government which emphasizes individual liberty and freedom, employs a system of checks and balances, and utilizes a bicameral legislature to ensure fair and equitable political outcomes to the benefit of all citizens. As a man, I understand why they do not care. As a soldier of a nation I have sworn to fight for, their indifference annoys me.

Our country, which I love dearly and of which I am a commissioned officer in its parachuting infantry forces, invaded this country, as one does, following a series of actions that took place over many centuries, culminating in one cataclysmic event which led to the scenario I am now describing to you. So I have been told. The details matter little. The details are tucked away in the passage of time, lost in allegiance to the living documents that represent our nation's system of governance. It is in fact both wise and prudent to leave such details buried as they are, never again to be found in the rat's nest of directives and orders that constitute the nature of an officer's duty to his nation.

My superior officers, as part of a larger plan to halt the flow of weapons and bombs into the country we successfully invaded, have emplaced me and my company of men at Combat Outpost Chemera with instructions to *disrupt* the enemy in our area of operations, or AO. However, and unfortunately for me and my men, our nation's leaders have decided that going into Gaumela in the hopes of, if not fully clearing Gaumela of insurgents, at least making them question their continued use of the village as a safe haven, might spur an international incident with the country pretending to not be at war. And we would never want to spark an international incident at this point in our invasion and occupation. But this does allow the insurgents to continue to launch volley after volley of rockets and mortars at our small compound from the safety afforded them by the border and the village of Gaumela. Which is unfortunate.

And an insurgent does in fact stand a pretty good chance of slipping by our meager patrols. We are one infantry company, 103 men, and we can only cover so much space at any given time. There is a lot of borderland, foothills, and mountains to *disrupt*. And we spend the majority of our time hunkered down in our frontier outpost absorbing these rocket salvos from across the border while simultaneously inhaling our ever-present burn pit smoke. These unfortunate burn pits—reported on, discussed, and written about over and over until they have become the defining feature of our generation's war—mark our various positions throughout the occupied country and will forever remain deep, dark scars across this land. These final resting places of our daily accumulation of trash, trash which includes our own shit and piss, is torched and burned each evening just before sunset. The effects of this action linger throughout the night and into the next day and all days thereafter, prodded, stoked, and renewed each evening to remind us of its presence just outside our gate and serving as backdrop for all my thoughts here in this country you have sent us to control until we become the burn pits themselves, tiny specks of flaming shit burning in a wasteland of our own creation.

The assault on the senses involved in this refuse-dumping chore of necessity—the hustle and bustle of disheveled, ill-disciplined soldiers, the acrid smell of burning lithium batteries, the clatter of assorted aluminum ammunition crates, the eye-watering stench of a days' worth of 103 men's accumulated waste—disturbs my evening constitutionals in and around the small combat outpost I am charged with commanding. This part of the soldier's life I can do without. A man should be allowed to enjoy a sunset without the smell of burning feces in his nostrils, without having to view the end of the daylight through the shimmering, burning remains of our material inefficiencies.

The first sergeant makes the argument that the late afternoon is the best time to dispose of the day's accumulated trash, that the men need to get all the chores around the outpost complete before posting themselves at their respective defensive positions for evening stand-to, a soldier's tradition of watching and guarding the outpost when the environmental conditions render him most vulnerable. So the batteries, ammunition dunnage, boxes of mail from anonymous well-wishers and supporters in our homeland, the shelf-stable food being compacted, pushed, and squeezed out of our intestines sizzles and cracks, smolders in its own toxicity each evening, as I cannot argue with the first sergeant's reasoning, nor can I offer an alternative schedule that makes sense for us all, at least not yet, because burning sh_t in the sunrise seems like an even worse alternative. But if we absolutely must produce all this trash we should bury it as deep in the earth as our conscience impels our labors to dig. We must dig so that future archeologists might learn something about our flawed present and apply it to their own special brand of flawed future in order to create tales of the past that fit the narrative of what will inevitably be their civilization's uniquely superior academic agendas.

Burn pits notwithstanding, I do bring up to my superiors the way in which we create a relatively small footprint across our area of operations, and that we absorb a lot of rockets that are being launched from across the border, and that we are not being provided all the tools and support needed to accomplish our herculean task, and that maybe, if we thought about it long enough, none of us, to include them, are being provided the proper tools and support needed to accomplish the mission. Their reply is always that our mere presence near the border is enough to have disruptive effects in the region, effects that reverberate beyond my area of operations and help support the larger war effort and that it is better to exercise restraint than to risk an international incident after you have invaded a country that turns out to be either indifferent to your system of governance or remains outright hostile to your proposed changes. This makes me feel better. Until *0500* the next morning when Combat Outpost Chemera is attacked once again by rockets from the vicinity of the village of Gaumela.

So when I ask my bosses if they have any other ideas as to how to reduce the barrage of exploding rockets my company regularly receives on Combat Outpost Chemera I am reminded that it is not necessarily the rockets that are of particular concern to them but the smuggling of bomb-making materials by the enemy further into the country. My superiors then proceeded to remind me that they believed if I would simply increase our patrol schedule to the point of ensuring a roughly fifty square kilometer AO was completely saturated with the presence of 103 infantrymen, then perhaps the rocket attacks would decrease. This idea is interesting, to say the least.

At the end of the day, though, I receive compensation for my work, and therefore do what my bosses tell me. At least most of the time. The bottom line is that as soldiers we fight where we are told. If provided the resources and a sufficient plan of action, the soldiers of our nation, a nation I love dearly, will always win. Always. So it once was, so it will ever be.

As a commissioned officer in the parachuting infantry forces of my nation, I possess a great deal of power, relatively speaking, if you happen to be one of those readers who believe the possession, distribution, and application of power is relative. Further, as part of my sacred duty as a commissioned officer, I view Combat Outpost Chemera as a sovereign part of our own country, an extension of our nation's belief systems, ethics, and cultural norms. Wherever I am deployed, whatever ground I stand upon, represents all for which our nation stands. Likewise, every patrol that walks out the front gate of Combat Outpost Chemera is a living, breathing representation of our country whose border reaches as far as the maximum effective range of each soldier's individual weapon systems. We are messengers carrying forth and delivering a foreign policy and unique idea of governance. Yet even with this power in my possession and with this mindset guiding the way in which we conduct business, we are routinely rocketed in the night and ambushed on patrol. What I have discovered is that when you are rocketed in the middle of the night while lying on your cot trying to read, it feels as if someone other than yourself is currently in possession of the power that, by rights of your successful invasion, belong to you. These midnight and early-morning rockets serve as a reminder that someone out there wants what we have and resents our projection of power. In time of war, then, it would seem that power is understood to be a zero-sum game. And power will not stand by and endure stalemate or stagnancy, at least not for more than twenty or so years before power loses interest and moves on to new projections.

Power moves, shifts, changes hands, and thrives in living waters, not stale, stagnant pools of forgotten backwater ponds. And these rockets that arrive while I am trying to think big-picture strategic thoughts, or sleep, or read a book, launched by those resentful of my peace of mind, a peace of mind only obtained because I have the power bestowed upon me by my affiliation with our nation and its inherent greatness, bother me. I do not wish to be bothered. I wish to be left alone to do my commanding and to do a little *disrupting* here and there in accordance with my directives.

We share the facilities at Chemera with a group of local border police, indigenous citizens of the nation we invaded who are responsible for border security. I have no idea how many of these men there are nor how many there are supposed to be. They come and go at their leisure. I have never watched them police anything. When they accompany us on patrols they seem to be overly friendly with the villagers, which is mildly off-putting. I do not know who enforces law and order in these villages. But someone does. Some invisible hand guides the actions of these mountain hovels. It is clearly not, however, this indigenous police force. My bosses push me to engage with these men, to train them, and to integrate them into our patrols; a clear exercise in futility. These men are incompetent as policemen and worse than incompetent as soldiers. The reality of our existence here on Combat Outpost Chemera is that we share very little, split down the middle as we are: their side and ours. If a more secure border exists on the planet than the one that divides Combat Outpost Chemera, I am not aware of it.

On occasion these men from the host nation hold a festive dance party on their side of the combat outpost, complete with food and musicians. They always invite me to these musical soirees and I will readily admit I do not mind attending, as the border policemen, completely clueless as to their professional function, are genuinely happy during these social get-togethers. They do need to borrow electric power from the generators on my side of the outpost for their lights, harmoniums, guitars, and microphones, however. So I suspect their desire for the convenience provided by my generators is the true reason for their invitation for me to join in the festivities. This does not upset me.

But this loaning of the use of our nation's power generators for our allied partners across the compound angers my soldiers. Our nation's soldiers have come to understand power as a finite commodity and see moving even a little generated electricity over to the other side of the combat outpost as somehow robbing them of their own full complement of power for the duration of the host nation soldiers' shindig. But I tell my soldiers to endure such slights against their military prowess and national supremacy for the evening because I enjoy seeing the men dance and enjoy each other's company in these moments of friendship, not caring about the fact that their country has been invaded and is now fighting an insurgency, and completely at ease with the knowledge that rockets occasionally rain down from across an international border just four or five kilometers away. This is, for now, the least I can do.

Naturally, rockets never rain down while the dance party is taking place. Maybe this is out of respect for the sanctity of the festivities. But let's be honest, the more likely scenario is that the men who typically fire rockets at the outpost just happen to also be in attendance at the dance party. It seems to me, though, that as long as these men are here dancing, they are not firing rockets nor smuggling additional arms and bombs across the border, so we are accomplishing our mission. They are *disrupted*. Unfortunately, when the party ends and all the lights, instruments, and microphones are unplugged and power is routed back to my side of the outpost, rockets will again land on Combat Outpost Chemera. This happens roughly forty-five minutes after the final notes are sung.

You may glean from this information what you will. This is my situation, both friendly and enemy. Sometimes we find it difficult to recognize when a description of a situation contains all the information required to complete our mission, and we ask for more and more details, more nuance, more description of the myriad factors that surround us, until explaining the situation becomes a mission in itself. And nothing is ever accomplished. We mark time talking and arguing about our individual protracted problems and the mire in which we find ourselves, and before we realize it, no doctrinal mission statement ever really gets written, much less the possibility of any sort of mission accomplishment, just a bunch of leaders milling about a country lamenting their lot in life, such as it is. Insurgencies grow, insurgencies that have always been there, brewing since our creation. This is the nature of war, each subordinate element a reflective microcosm of the larger effort, so that fighting these various insurgencies on a grand scale becomes the fighting of insurgencies on myriad smaller scales, until one day you wake up to find an insurgency on your own outpost or within your own deep-seated loyalties.

History shows us that these situations have always been created from the top down and then fought from the bottom up. But the situation must be viewed at the lowest level possible, a graphic representation of our anatomy, and our choices, as seen from the first moments of our creation. Only then can we properly see the fight taking place all along right under our noses, the true fight that occurs from the bottom up, as all fights must. Tie the two together and you might have yourself a mission statement worth fighting for. Tie the two together and a mission statement may no longer be necessary. Because right now as I tell you this and ponder what it is to have you call me, all I really want is to watch an unfiltered sunset, to have one singular moment unimpeded by burn-pit smoke in my eyes and the smell of burning shit in my nose.

2.

THE SOLDIERS GATHERED HERE at Combat Outpost Chemera's burn pit serve the collective good of what we mostly assume is a grateful nation. The men here are individual shit stirrers in the grand detail of military service. They play grab-ass the way soldiers do, the way soldiers always have, the way soldiers always will. Rock-throwing games of skill. Wrestling to the edge of the burn pit. Lighting of flatulence. Shit-on-a-stick games. They rarely speak to me during my evening strolls, perhaps out of respect for and understanding of my need to brood. Perhaps out of respect for my position of authority. Perhaps respect runs both ways. Or perhaps this is a byproduct of me not saying anything to them, shutting off communication by enforcing the boundary between officer and enlisted man through my actions, slowly patrolling the grounds with my little notebook and a look of authority. They think I am working on the next mission plan while I think they are simply playing grab-ass around a burn pit. We are both wrong.

I am not sure I would hear them even if they did say anything to me directly, at least not cognizantly. Excessive and unnecessary noise typically bothers me. But a setting sun has a magical way of blanketing the world in stillness, even when viewed dimly through the dark glass of our lives here. There's a calm to the proceedings, a neat ordering of the day, a clearing out of accumulated refuse to make room for the night. Superfluous, unnecessary noise is slowly sucked behind the horizon with the daylight. Even with the disruptions at this unfortunate pit, a fellow may, with the right mindset and a little effort, block out the flurry of activity and clear his head as he completes his evening inspections around the outpost. I can conduct my constitutional with a vague sense of normalcy forgetting for just a moment what I am and what I will forever be. I will not change. Neither will these soldiers. Neither will this pit.

Back inside the compound, I make my way through rows of hastily constructed squad huts cobbled together with thin plywood, flimsy doors that will not fully close, stacks of sandbags for stairs in lieu of ones never built, all indicators of lowest-bid construction work conducted by local contractors eager for a lucrative contract from our guilt-ridden invading army's uncanny ability to throw money at a problem. The big three-sided barn in the center of the outpost—not really a barn in the traditional sense but I call it a barn anyway, pretending this is an old fort, the wild, wild West of our homeland—beckons in the distance. The barn serves as a gathering place for my ideas and the place I scribble, jot down, and organize most of my thoughts on pressing matters at hand so that I might better understand my place here. I move through the compound as all army officers move in these situations, milling about, pretending to inspect things, putting on airs of a hierarchic presence, a technique born out of a self-conscious desire to look commanding in some way, stopping just long enough in one place to take in as much of the distant mountain landscape as I can without looking sentimental, without seeming fruity for a sunset, as if searching for an item right in front of me yet deliberately avoiding it.

The big barn houses the company's rations, water, and excess gear, but more importantly it offers several inviting places to sit back and enjoy a cigarette. I open my aluminum case, take a cigarette out, and light the tobacco with a single match from an MRE matchbook, an achievement in the soft evening breeze, before heading inside the barn and taking my place on an empty ammo crate. The occasional, peaceful affectation of a smoke proves a comforting punctuation to my evening walks. This one is especially pleasant, each inhale a miniature acupuncturist at work on my throat. The deep inhales elicit increased pleasure and relaxation, each drag carries with it the soothing, audible sound of lung-damaging conspicuous consumption and pure momentary pleasure. Hazy, snow-capped mountains in the east creep closer with each inhale as if being physically drawn to me with each painful breath, inching their way to me with every deep, eye-crinkling inhalation of tobacco until the mountains are wholly familiar to me once again.

You know these mountains. You have visited these same mountains in our homeland. Or in your own travels abroad. Because all mountains are the same. When you silently stare at these mountains long enough they will offer up a warming light within, a connection you can feel deep in your soul. This light longs to be acknowledged, longs for unity within you, and begs to know why you have drifted so far, why you have smothered and distanced that which burns within, beckons that inside you which you recognize as fallen. And still, the names of these mountains escape you even now because once you see with your eyes what in the past has only been felt you begin to recognize this truth: names don't matter in this moment. All you want to know now is the warmth of the light inside you, and so you breathe deeper so the light might gain fuel from the cool air. And the mountains move closer. Much of the time, this light will escape us, leaving us to hide away in mountains, in forests, in rivers, in deserts, and in the stars above, in homes and hearts, taunting and torturing as the light that should be within begs us to follow from a distance. And as we chase the light we will soon find that all these transient places are the same, only the trees serve as indicators that we are someplace we do not belong, someplace in which we are slowly being extinguished.

I am introspective this evening, a state of emotion I actively seek in these evening constitutionals but that mostly alludes me. This brooding suits me in the brisk air of the evening, a briskness that arrives sooner than expected. I will not be moved from this silence. Sitting here in the big barn each evening while the men stand at 100 percent security just prior to and just after sundown is preventive medicine, a breaking up of life here, a separation from the men, if only for the sunrise and the sunset. These stand-tos are conducted daily—a soldier's morning and evening prayer—every guard tower manned, every soldier on full alert, awaiting an insurgent attack. The enemy, any enemy, every enemy since the dawn of time, attacks just before dawn and just after sunset when visibility is lowest and a soldier's night vision, and the usefulness of his night vision goggles, are least effective. That is what we are told in our battle histories. So soldiers practice this ancient tradition passed down from generation to generation like so many other traditions of fighting men.

Thoughts here in the barn consist mostly of my longing for my own hideaway, a private place with just enough garden to sustain me and my family. There are goats for milk and cheese, and chickens scratching in the dirt searching for a sustaining connection to the earth. A wife, younger, sturdy, and hardy. And children. Children running around the yard barefoot. Children at play on a homemade swing hung from a reliable, welcoming tree. A home represents a man's soul, his contemplative sheltering space, the act of sticking a chicken's head under its wing and rocking it to sleep, a soothing safehaven in a hidden valley of mountains I can reach out and touch but cannot name. The mountains are everywhere and nowhere even as you read this. And there is nothing else. No distractions. Only the intense longing that comes from knowing something is missing, something to which you must return.

It's been four days since our last rocket attack and at least two weeks since one took place in the evening. When the air is sufficiently still and quiet, as it is now, only the intermittent seasonal breezes break the calm, and you can hear the rounds of the rockets ripping towards you, slicing through the thin, high-desert air. And as the rocket alarm begins its loud screech this cool evening a mere second before the first round lands just outside the compound, and the men begin their shouts of *incoming*, scramble for cover, and hunker down in their towers and bunkers, I hold fast to my position in the barn and wait for the next rounds to arrive, betting my life on their ineffectiveness yet feeling their reverberations in the soles of my boots. The mountains instantly return to their place in geographic space as I feign collected coolness and cling to my now disrupted silence. This is what our war has become, a series of guessing games and prayers as to when and where the rockets will next land or trying to figure out when and where the earth will spontaneously explode beneath us.

What follows is the cacophony of sergeants running around, checking equipment, getting head counts, the NCOs doing what they do best, the standard drill that takes place to check and see if this was the volley in which tragedy strikes. Not this time though. Not today. But soon.

I stick my head out of the comfort of the barn and see the first sergeant striding through the compound accounting for the men.

"I'm over here, First Sergeant."

"Gotcha, sir."

"All good, I presume?"

"Yeah, we're good."

He starts to head over and I interrupt him.

"I'm going to hang out here a bit longer. Just let the XO know when we're 100 percent so he can send the report. I'll be in in a bit for my phone call with the boss."

"Okay, sir. Need anything?"

"No, First Sergeant. I'm good. Thanks."

He heads back the other direction, completely kitted up in body armor and helmet, nine-millimeter strapped to his side, fully in his element.

3.

A SENSE OF CALM after the storm of rockets settles over the compound and I am happy to stay put and out of the way for the time being. Absorbing enemy rockets to no effect, and the subsequent aftermath, does not require a command presence. So as I sit and go over the upcoming patrol schedules, future missions, and what of today should be reported during the nightly phone call with my boss back at Camp Palermo, I begin to think about a game of make-believe I started playing when I was a young boy. I was probably ten years old when the game started. If you know of this game of mine and how it played out it may help shed light on my life and career, such as it is, and my choices, such as they are.

I invented the game while alone in my room with the door locked. This was my way. The window in my room overlooked a neighboring orchard of apples and pears, and as I sat and stared at the perfectly-formed rows of fruit trees, I began to formulate a game of baseball players and their statistics that quickly grew into an obsession I carried throughout my youth and into adulthood until my first combat experience, at which point the game came to a halt. War strips you of childhood games. At least what you think war will be. At least what war has become.

I do not know what has made me think of the game now, sitting on an ammo crate, smoking a cigarette, taking incoming rockets and mortars on a compound five kilometers from an international border between two countries, pondering my life in the present by holding this moment against the past in search of an unknowable future. I have been here in this country, perhaps even in this barn, if you can understand this, many times before, and to understand this is to understand that I have always been here since my creation and that I will likely always be here in one way or another. And in this truth you may begin to see the memories of childhood games as nothing more than reflections on the forging of the spirit that takes place deep within and ultimately leads to the chasing after the romance of war in the defense of our nation. This is what I tell myself in hopes that it will help you see the truth.

My invented game took place in the margins of notebooks, textbooks, and journals, anything with available space in which to play out my fantasy game. Baseball, of course, used to be considered our nation's national pastime. I do not think this is the case anymore, as most of our fellow citizens have moved beyond the delicate pacing, attention to detail, and geometric comprehension required of the game in favor of the immediate gratification offered by sports they feel capture the essence of battle despite their lack of any knowledge of what actually constitutes warfare. Today's modern citizen requires a meticulously staged yet inherently flawed image of violence played out before them which will curb the bloodlust they so desperately cling to but would never participate in themselves, preferring to send professional soldiers to do the unpleasant work of soldiering. This transition away from a cerebral game to a game representing something more violent was inevitable in the structure of our society, so it does not bother me. But I have always preferred the game of baseball, even to this day.

The players in my creation were held up against players of the past whose numbers are, or at least at one time were, generally understood to be the traditional numbers of greatness as we have come to know them historically: 755, 714, or 536 career home runs, 200 hit seasons, 4191 hits, and lifetime batting averages over .300. This was my game. A game of make-believe invented while alone in my room seeking an alternate reality in which to hang what I understood to be truth against the fantasy world slowly unveiling itself to me throughout my adolescence and into adulthood.

I scribbled and scratched these invented season statistics over a fictional player's career on any paper I might find in my hands, a world of numbers squeezed into the margins, a collection of statistics bleeding across the paper's ill-defined and poorly secured borders, a secret parallel world of my own devising and the manifest destiny of my will to conquer anywhere I found open space. Wherever I saw an opening, a void to be filled, no matter how big or small, I filled it with my game of make-believe, a projection of my power to create, and a game dependent solely on the efficacy of statistics to elucidate a man's contribution to his team.

Every schoolteacher I ever had, every staff meeting or training I ever attended as a young up-and-coming soldier, I must have appeared to be the most diligent of note-takers, as I kept my head buried in my notebook, appearing to take notes. But I was only half-listening to the proceedings and nodding in affirmation based on the rise and fall of the voices I barely heard in the surrounding din as player after player came to fruition in notebook after notebook in the building of my pre-combat empire. If asked a question directly—to elucidate a point, give an opinion, or provide feedback—I could literally hear the crack of the bat in my head and an announcer's excited words as I thumbed through my papers and notes pretending to look for an answer that was not there but that I would somehow manage to provide:

He got all of that one! Back, back, way back, he is definitely tracking this answer, ladies and gentlemen, and he's only been half-listening! Not even trying. Effortless. How does he do it? What a game for the ages!

Then I spoke and gave a mostly satisfactory answer:

"Ummm . . . I see the monster in the book as a blank slate to be imprinted upon by society."

Or once out of school and in my pre-combat, early years of service to our nation:

"Our third-quarter marksmanship numbers are up, sir, and . . . uhhh . . . we are 100 percent fully mission capable."

Because I was busy inventing players in the marginalia I failed to take any real notes save for the most important aspects of a meeting. My notebooks were 90 percent marginalia, 10 percent useful content, a ratio that renders useless the meaning of the words. The marginalia was the content, and the meeting notes, what should have been a tether to reality, were ephemeral doodles possessing meaning only so long as they served as reminders of the excruciating minutiae of my day-to-day life, a dropped anchor for the purposes of what I am being told is an important daily chore only to be quickly pulled up again in order to set sail across the seas of creation. The effect these tasks exerted on my life would then flutter away as they opened up new pages, new seasons, new players, another conglomerate of statistics to guide my baseball compositions. The only information in my notebooks and textbooks that truly mattered was on the fringes, along the border, pushed to the edge of the pages by the order of the life in which I found myself an unwilling yet fully capable participant. The mindless tedium that should have constituted detailed notes became pointless drivel:

> —*Who is truly bad? The monster or mankind? Re: I am malicious because I am miserable. Essay due next Friday.*

Or once out of school and in the early stages of my military career:

> —*Uniform inspection next Monday.*
> —*ASAP: Turn in range slides to S3.*

The roots of this game took place after I read a book called *Baseball's 100 Greatest Players*. I do not remember the name of the writer of the book but do recall that it was published by Good Sports Press. I knew when I was ten, the age at which I first read this book, that unless baseball ceased to exist the moment the book was published, then the list was pointless, outdated the moment it left the printers and a new season started. Players of the past would move up and down the chart based on the performance of players in the present and the start of each new season begins the process of eradicating the list's usefulness if even by the smallest of incremental changes in the accumulation of numbers.

In his defense, the author stated in the preface that this was his own personal list based on his findings and his own established standards of excellence, though I am not convinced this absolves him of the sin of compiling a list of baseball's greatest player which cannot actually exist in any real way. I do not know if the book is still available or if Good Sports Press still exists and if they do that they still publish books that bring into question the concepts of time and space like *Baseball's 100 Greatest Players*. But if the book can be found now, some thirty years later, we would see how pointless the book actually was, the passage of substantial time now making obvious what was clear to me at ten years old.

Yet despite the book's inability to properly grapple with the nature of time and space in the universe, the book still provided the framework of baseball numbers that would serve as a guide for the remainder of my life. *Baseball's 100 Greatest Players* could only exist, for better or worse in my development, as a frozen moment in baseball history in which concrete standards of excellence were established and would forever remain. A reality grounded only in the present and which would shape my view of all baseball history. The actual game of baseball, as it exists in real time and space in our nation, continues to move, progress, and evolve as the game's relationship to our world changes, and can even devolve into irrelevance, as we are now seeing take place.

Nevertheless, I have always considered the standards for excellence in the game to remain unchanged. The standards and their associated numbers, are all that matter, not who or what constitutes a fluid list of ever-changing names moving up and down an arbitrary ranking. To this day, insomuch as I ever think about a game that was once considered our nation's national pastime, nothing anyone says or does can change these sacred numbers in my head. At the age of ten, time ceased to progress in my baseball mind forever. Baseball's reality existed on a separate plane of existence within the marginalia that constituted my life, the whitespace filled with numbers based on the concrete reality of standards provided in an otherwise useless book of rankings. These statistical doodles accounted for the nature of my existence, frozen in time, an imaginary civilization found inside a game of numbers.

I cannot replicate the numbers in my made-up game now, as I am currently in the post-combat chapter of my life and therefore no longer able to engage in imaginary games of player creation. Despite the game's call to me, despite the personal destiny I felt the game fulfilled in me as a lonely boy who spent many hours alone in an adolescent bedroom starring at an orchard and pondering the meaning of life, once I tasted combat for the first time the game lost the ability to hold my interest. The whitespace in my days could no longer be filled with imaginary at-bats, runs, hits, and home runs of invented baseball players, but instead began to be filled with geometric patterns, triangulations, the angles and symmetry that create battlefield scenarios in which there are no sides, only left and right limits, minimum safe distances, and maximum effective ranges of various weapon systems facing each other on the field of battle. The old web of creation I had built fell by the wayside and a new reality was borne within. Yet the truth we now know was always there, idly taking notes just outside the border of prescribed space, surreptitious creations under the nose of reality.

And so I find myself here now, thinking of this childhood game and getting up off my seat in the barn to begin my walk around the compound during what remains of stand-to. I shift my thoughts to tomorrow's mission, or yesterday's mission, or last year's plethora of operations, milling about my outpost, in charge of everything I survey and still trying to escape the burn pit that exposes our weakness as a conquering civilization. What I am presenting to you is an initial image, an image of my making, an image of a realist, not bent on superfluous gestures of shallow, patriotic virtue-signaling but in finding the truth, like someone else's truth that just landed with a roiling, thunderous explosion just outside our compound.

I have found over the years that military leadership should match the situation onto which it is forced to practice. And I believe this applies to the way in which we tell our stories as well. We project ourselves—as the one creating the words, as leaders in the marketing of truth—onto a situation as seen from a distance and then paint a picture that elucidates all the myriad ways in which we can, together, achieve our end state. Strategies, methods, and functions—or tactics, techniques, and procedures—should be derived from the utilization of finely tuned senses found deep within the true fighting man and his desire to do nothing more than help his team, to help the citizens around him from the bottom up, from deep within the recesses of his soul and then to project these skills outward in an ever-expanding maximum effective range of internal systems of thought and function and newfound hopes and dreams in an attempt to intersect with the fellow fighting men to his left and right.

This is an exhausting process. So to carry out this mission, the leader must steal a little time for himself, contemplate his mission and his duty to his fellow man, separate himself from the fray momentarily, continually affirm the hierarchy that, out of necessity for strong leadership, places him at the top of the food chain in his piece of the organization, a place of power he must continually justify both to himself and to his fellow citizens. He must find within himself the driving force that makes him who he is, reconcile this warrior's spirit and come to terms with his existence as a soldier and what a leader of men should be. The lonely, monastic existence executed by men who feel something deep within that further separates them from the rest of the world should not be burdened with the latest *power-of-positive-leadership feel-good* book being marketed this month. War is not a one-size-fits-all proposition nor is it a production line to be picked apart and analyzed in the hopes of obtaining streamlined efficiency. War is a complex entity unto itself and deserves to be treated as such. We are not in the business of engineering the most efficient delivery of mass marketed products to a comatose clientele. We are here in the service of our nation, a nation we all love deeply, in an effort to kill other human beings, and to bend those we do not kill to accept our way of thinking. If we are not prepared to embrace this reality then we are in the wrong line of work. If we are not prepared to trust that every single man on the ground and every single leader views the battlefield from a different angle unique to him, then we can never win. We are sounding a siren to which no one will heed, telling a story in which no one will listen.

4.

DURING STAND-TO ALL THE generators in the compound are turned off save one keeping the headquarters' computers and radios powered, the loud din of rumbling electrical power reduced to a faint hum in the distance. Not total silence but close. A door has been left open in the headquarters building, allowing a tiny sliver of light into the creeping dark. I walk directly from the barn and across the compound to shut the offending door, my eyes readjusting as I step out of the dark shade and into the gray night sky to shut the flimsy door and take one more lap around the compound, make sure no one is still hunkered down in bunkers—laugh at them if they are—before heading back to the headquarters building for my nightly update with the boss and then finally on to my room for the night.

A thin line of resilient sunset clings to the horizon, refusing to cede its waning power to the night. This land has long ago learned to wait in the stillness of time, long ago learned that the earth will continue to move, and that even the sun cannot control or conquer the people in these deserts, these mountain ranges, these raging rivers and wadis and lush forests and alpine meadows and foothills, regardless of who crosses their borders, borders they care little about.

The final, meandering lap to check on the soldiers who have drawn the guard shift directly after stand-to—hands-down the best guard shift—proves largely uneventful. Generators spark up again around the compound and the regular arguments can be heard over who has next shift, who is getting screwed, and when so-and-so last pulled guard. A low, panicked rumble of a discussion over whose rifle was left in the tower spills into the air:

"Whose fucking weapon is this?"

"Check the serial number."

"Jeez-us Christ."

"Fucking piece of shit."

A soldier still in full uniform streaks by me in the dark, his panic real, though I cannot imagine how a soldier would come to leave his personal weapon in a guard tower in this environment. Extenuating circumstances perhaps. A series of comic events involving multiple primary and secondary weapon systems perhaps. The same old same old. On repeat.

Security is maintained on Combat Outpost Chemera at 25 percent, at least on paper. Soldiers mostly nap in guard towers or work out some internal rotation system in which 25 percent really just turns out to be, at best, 10 percent. And 10 percent security is fine. Which is why I set nightly guard at 25 percent. Some battles are lost before they begin, and I find it best to sometimes turn a blind eye to malfeasance, for the betterment of the team—or to keep up appearances.

Peering into the darkness at the shanties that make up the local border police contingent's housing and headquarters on the other side, I see only a few dim, still lights—no sounds, no arguments, no confusion—like looking into a distant spiraling arm of our own galaxy, connected, yet still so far away. One would think the border police already asleep were it not for the occasional shadow moving across the face of the huts delivering trays of tea and rice and bread, an evening game show in which the contestant must deliver sustenance to the occupants of primitive dwellings under the pressure of the clock. I feel responsible for them, in the way I have been trained, though they remain a complete unknown to me. They operate, if this is the right word for what they do, quietly, efficiently, in a pitch-black protective swirling of silence that is their way. In terms of soldering skills they are woefully incompetent. But I trust them and think they mean well. And they host a good dinner and dance party.

Back on our own side, streaking blurs of nighttime activity flood the night with red-lensed headlamps and pen lights creating chaos out of what should be solitude, soldiers moving between huts for God only knows what. One hundred three men of my nation, volunteers all, three platoons and a headquarters, thrust together on a tiny fortress of mud and rock in the middle of nowhere, here to finish a job started many, many years ago with no end in sight. How does this look from the border police side of the compound? I cannot know. I am not on their side.

The people of this land have survived invasions before, weathered thousands of years of fighting, sent kings and generals away with hubristic tails tucked between their legs. The people of this land have created their own borders, built a wall of resentment dividing them from all others. Caring why past nations have failed in their efforts to conquer serves no purpose. The point is moot. I volunteered my body and brain and talents and skills to be an infantryman and a paratrooper, not a foreign policy expert, historian, or anthropologist. Give me the tools with which to do my job and the agreed-upon compensation and I will do my duty to the best of my ability. This is all you can ask of a soldier.

This land however this terrain, this way of life, saps a soldier's strength. Each new day wears down the resolve required to win a protracted war. The slow movement of time chips away at the senses little by little until nothing is left but the blurred memories of past skirmishes, small scrapes here and there, the sound of bullets ricocheting off rocks, the sting of dirt swirling and blowing across a blistered face, the futile excursions into endless networks of high mountain caves, and the endless waiting for time to pause for just a second, to punctuate the incessant ticking with one loud resonating gong to remind us why we exist. We are waiting for time to make the first move. To *disrupt*. These moments recur in the soldier's head in a loop until no one knows where they are anymore or how long they have been in this place—one long, continuous memory punctuated by the smell of two thousand years of burning shit. These timelines make no sense to a combat-trained eye. Because your last firefight was always your most ferocious. Your last unit was always your best unit. What is viewed as the present mediocrity exists as a pale simulacrum of your past, a story told in the pages of journals and diaries and hastily scrawled stories that only tell half the truth, only tell you what you want to hear.

The infantrymen of Chemera continue their nightly rush in the darkness attending to their evening personal duties post-stand-to. One soldier tunes his guitar, hiding himself away between squad huts so as to not be disturbed. Soldiers will always find a way to get their most cherished possessions across the sea and into a land of violence. This thought satisfies me. Other soldiers start card games, the shouting and arguing before the first hand is dealt ricochets around the compound. A few run to the showers still fully dressed, towels and shower kit in tow, a race to be the first to lay claim to what little hot water is available. A dedicated few go back to work readying their personal equipment, cleaning weapons under a squad leader's watchful eye, brushing off their gear, restocking food and water for the *tick-tock, tick-tock* that constitutes the next day's mission.

The large wooden building that makes up the living quarters for the headquarters platoon as well as the medic's aid station and the company operations center remains a calming presence in a dark, turbulent sea. Across the front of the building extends a porch from end to end. A single plywood door on the far end serves as entrance to my small captain's quarters. I am the only one on the compound with the privacy afforded by my own space. Many commanders would have turned down the private space, made an altruistic gesture to demonstrate that he was just *one of the boys*, and that the room would be better utilized for medical supplies or personal gear storage. But a commander needs separation from the men he commands. No one wants to see the man that will lead them over the hill or order them to charge a machine gun nest baby-wiping his testicles before bed. No one wants to see their commander awkwardly getting changed, his private business flopping around, pale ass shining for the world to see, after a cold shower. Why pretend to be one of them when I am very clearly not? Many commanders become too comfortable with their subordinates. A leader should know he is set apart, and he should know *they know* he is different. Men need leaders, not just another guy in a towel hopping around the dirty, pube-and-toenail infested floor in flip-flops trying to put his pants on over still-wet legs without toppling over, just another man pissing in a bottle in the middle of the night just like them. Nor does a commander want to make judgments about his men based on which ones have to be instructed in the basic use of shower shoes, which soldiers puts their tops on before their bottoms, and which soldiers do not understand that there are other entertainments in the world beside pornography and comic book movies. And anyway, after eighteen years of service, more than anyone else on the compound, had I not earned a bit of privacy? I have been a private. I have reached the upper echelons of the non-commissioned officer ranks. And then I started all over by becoming a commissioned officer and a lowly lieutenant. Do I not deserve a space to call my own if I can get it? I will let you, dear reader, be the judge of such sentiments.

These quarters are my sanctuary, my nest, and my nook. Protection from the fray. Entering my room, I take off my boots and lie perfectly still in my cot, basking in the soothing emptiness. If I stay like this I will soon fall into a deep slumber, and it is much too early for sleep. Propping myself on an elbow I turn on my reading lamp and lean across the big trunk which serves as both storage for my personal effects and makeshift desk. I grab the notebook in which I scribble the notes—events, dialogues, actions—of the day. I do not call this a journal, though that is what it surely is. It is *my book*, such as it is, my letter to someone else, in another time and another place, as all books truly are.

In my quarters I also keep someone else's book, a work I have been slowly making my way through, a book about whalers in vengeful pursuit of a great beast, a subject I know nothing about. But I do know that the ship's captain does not sleep in the hull with the men he commands. That would be unseemly. But once my own daily thoughts and events are put down into my book, I open up someone else's book and begin my nightly reading.

There is comfort to be had in reading about events far removed from one's own lot in life, and yet there is a similar comfort in knowing that the characters in this book about whaling see the sun rise and set on the same scene every day, day in and day out, a continual, unchanging existence. The details are inconsequential. The monotony of sameness drives the narrative, one mission pursued at the expense of all else—home, family, friends, a sense of self. A man has one purpose. He must find that purpose and pursue it with every fiber of his being. Even if it kills him. If he fails in this, he is liable to let little things irritate him and get the best of him. He will grow unpleasant and taciturn. Perhaps worse. His failures will gnaw at him, forcing him to withdraw to another place deep inside his psyche, never to be found again, lost in the depths of his sense of vengeance. And his ship will travel round and round the seas lost in its own pursuit, sunk in time's ever-expanding maw, being drawn closer and closer in an ever-shrinking whirlpool that represents the whaler's demise.

Launched into the unknown worlds found in my book about whaling I read the same paragraphs over and over, entire pages even, before snapping out of a daydream—a childhood event, a relationship gone wrong, a recent tactical scenario I was working through, or replaying a past firefight in my head—before realizing not a single word has been retained. Eventually a blind acceptance of this skimming process takes place, an acceptance of the words on the page as nothing more than a metronomic device designed to rock me into a sense of comfort and security. The story no longer matters, if it ever did; what matters is the words themselves acting as buffers to my thinking reality, a balm to take my mind off the present and transport me to a place where I know nothing, the chaos of unknown worlds, a sea of knowledge dissolving into the comfort of watery blankness, the security of my own thoughts on repeat. A man can find solace in the realization that he does not know everything, nor is he required to.

Many of my fellow officers read books about war, military histories, strategy. But why read about war when you are in the middle of one? Such endeavors make a leader narrow-minded and unimaginative in strategic practice. Soldiers should read about subjects for which they possess no frame of reference, like whaling, elaborate courtships, the memory of childhood smells, or poetry. This is what makes a well-rounded soldier and prepares him for the ensuing disorder. I know nothing of the sea. I know nothing of a sailor's knots. I know nothing of jibs and mainsails. Yet I know exactly what is taking place. I become anchored in this mystical unknown. My reality transfers to the page and I am on a tall ship chasing a great leviathan. Burn pit stench becomes salty air, the trash pit is now slaughtered hunks of sperm whale piling up on the ship's deck, my small room an angry sea captain's quarters. The pursuit is a mystical journey and all end states are the same. On such nights I enjoy dreamless slumber, deep and undisturbed, safe in the berth of my cocoon only to repeat the entire process again tomorrow, just as it has been repeated for thousands of years before I ever made an appearance in this fallen land.

5.

THE SOUND OF SOLDIERS in the next room wakes me, my reading lamp still on, book sitting open across my chest. I bring my watch into the light to make out the time. *0440*. The heaviness of unmotivated boots shuffling across dusty floors echoes through the thin-walled building. Accumulation of a night's farts and snores congregate, cloud-like, forming a thick, mood-altering haze of indignation for the soldier's lot in life before slipping into my room to fully wake me from my stupor.

There is nothing special about today. Another patrol in another village, a village we have been to several times already. *Disrupting*. I have been here before, this place, with these men, on this mission. I have been in this room for many years now, it would seem. On this loop since my nation first sent us here so many years ago. My captain's berth buckles and sways with activity as the headquarters platoon begins to get up and move around spurred by the flurry of activity outside and the line platoon soldiers who make it a habit of traipsing through the building just to make sure the lazier headquarter soldiers are awake.

One of my biggest fears in this, my third, maybe my fourth, deployment to this land my nation conquered is the false sense of security that comes with repetitive monotony. I am guilty of it myself, and often catch myself asking soldiers if they are ready for the *big* mission, unable to hide the dry sarcasm in my voice. But soldiers have been killed taking the same route back to their camp after a patrol. Platoons get ambushed when a single far side security decides to eat their MRE rather than stay focused on the crest of a blind spot protecting the main elements flank. So each patrol must be special, every mission the most important mission ever conducted. Maintenance at that level of required energy does not come easy.

"Don't get complacent, men."

"Head on a swivel."

"It's when you least expect it that the enemy strikes."

Well, then, we must always expect it, shouldn't we? Until an empty, blank space forms where there should be power and strength. And when a part of you dries up, goes missing, it must be replaced with affectation. These are the stories we tell ourselves at *0446* in the morning just prior to another mission.

My maps, kit, and assorted gear are laid out, prepped for the day, and I sit contemplating a shave and a venture to the mess tent for coffee. The shave will wait. The increasing grey of my stubble provides a look of gravitas and wisdom that endears me to the locals anyway. We convince ourselves of many things to account for indifference. And laziness.

Over the years of our nation's penchant for war the soldier's load has increased exponentially based on defense contractors' ability to sell our army a growing mound of clothing, gear, and technology ill-suited for a soldier of any stripe, much less soldiers expected to fight in these rugged mountains and deserts. To even go out on a two- or three-day-long mission now requires at least six Meals-Ready-to-Eat, an ungodly amount of water, countless batteries, sleep systems, clothing configurations for nearly every weather contingency, and more changes of socks and t-shirts than entire expeditions would have carried as they settled and explored our home country's frontier in centuries prior. Not to mention the radios, lasers, night vision, and scopes with which we are now burdened. But *travel light, freeze at night*, I say.

I set my stripped-down, minimalist gear outside my door—helmet, M4 carbine with old-school iron sights, body armor with magazine chest rig and two side pouches for a water bottle and a notepad, a small assault pack containing a poncho, map, compass, a few markers, some snacks, one MRE, cigarettes, night vision device, a few spare batteries to help lighten the load for my radioman, and my journal—which goes with me everywhere and which doubles as my notebook on operations—and walk over to the mess tent for coffee, stopping to relieve myself at one of the many overused and outdated piss-tubes still scattered around the compound, despite the dedicated metal shit-bucket latrines installed by a previous unit several years prior to our arrival.

The two platoons headed out today are already making their way to the mouth of the serpentine dirt walls that lead to our front gate squad-by-squad depending on the attitude of the individual squad leader's demeanor and the subsequent adjustment of reporting times for each subordinate element down the line. Once they get to the dirt walls, they will sit. And wait. This is the way armies have always operated, and I am sure even ancient troops, particularly lowly privates, have spent most of their time sitting on their asses, some probably on this exact piece of terra firma.

"Morning, sir."

"What's up, sir?"

"'Nuther big mission, eh, sir?"

I meet each morning greeting with a deep throated *morning, 'sup,* or *oh yeah* as I make my way into the mess tent, fill up my big mug and head back to the operations center, swinging by to grab my gear sitting outside my door on the way. The executive officer is already at his designated corner of the room when I walk in. He says nothing to me, just yawns and goes about his business while digging sleep out of his eyes.

I put down my gear and sit at my desk sipping my coffee in silence, pretending to review some notes that were left on my desk from several missions back that have nothing to do with today's work.

0527. Get kitted up and start my move to the front gate. The XO desperately wants me to ask him about the reports so he can answer with an air of *how dare anyone question my competence* but I refuse to give him the satisfaction and, when done kitting up, I only ask if he will meet us at the front gate to get a headcount on our way out.

"Of course, sir. And the reports are already sent up to Battalion."

I stiffen and embrace the day ahead, snatching up my helmet and my rifle together in my right hand and march out of the building with a slow, purposeful gait.

"Thanks, XO."

The soldier hum, that boiling rumble of conversations, jokes, and pre-combat inspections designed to kill time and keep each other awake, remains a signatory event in the patrol process, a sign that the art of tension-building has now begun in earnest and the next steps in the process must be handled delicately in order to set the conditions for a quality patrol. If I arrive for my pre-patrol pep talk too soon the soldiers barely have enough time to catch their breath after spending the morning running around, being yelled at, and inspected ad nauseam. The hum needs time to develop. But if I wait too long, boredom will set in, and no amount of speechification can rouse a soldier once boredom has set in. The tone and volume of the soldier's hum must be judged for just the right moment to enter the scene.

I move through the gaggle of soldiers near the front entryway to Combat Outpost Chemera, gathering a sense of the mood, building within myself the sense of destiny required to embrace the full force of my duties and what it means to be a soldier and a leader in this moment.

In my head I am a cavalry troop commander from our nation's early frontier days, mounting my trusty steed, holding my saber across the naked pommel of my saddle. My paint mare has to be reined almost continuously as she high-steps through columns of my fellow frontier soldiers eagerly awaiting my leadership. A dusty, well-worn Stetson, wide brim upturned, rests jauntily atop my head. A long, red scarf flaps in the breeze.

0550. As is the standard in the company, the squad leaders and lieutenants move to the front of the gathering soldiers while the platoon sergeants stay in the back. In normal conversation I am slow and calculating, polite but not gregarious or friendly, each word simmering in the weight of its own definition, coming out thoughtfully, with a purpose. Some may find my conversation too studied, ensuring each word is clearly articulated, understood, and explained to the point of exhaustion. However, a different technique must be adopted in military briefings or pre-misson speeches. The theatrics often outweigh the words themselves, resulting in a distracting drama to which I am often completely oblivious as to the words themselves. It is entertainment and exactly what soldiers need before stepping off on a mission. Now is not the time to issue details or critical information. Now is the time to put on the soldier's disposition, provide an overview, a mere idea of the day's events, the defining tone of our raison d'etre.

Imagining myself moving back and forth in front of my men on my high-stepping horse, their rapt attention focused on me as the breaking morning lends weight to a speech designed to do nothing more than let them know their leader is here and ready for action I begin my speech with a loud, stentorian tone that lets everyone know to pay attention:

"Gentlemen! We have a job to do today. What say we do it!?"

A series of hoots and hollers fills the morning air in response.

"We have our orders. Find the enemy. Disrupt the enemy. First Platoon, half of you will be on the higher ground of our southern flank with me, and other half will parallel the wadi to the north of the route under the command of your platoon leader. The first sergeant will remain with this group."

I point in each direction with my saber as I give these instructions, twisting and turning in my saddle as the lively mare dances and turns in front of the men.

"Second platoon, you'll march with squads in column giving yourself plenty of room between elements—traveling overwatch, I say—in case some ignorant fool of an insurgent should think himself brave enough to attack our formidable element. Those of us on the flanks will utilize successive bounds to protect and overwatch each element. Now . . . today and all days . . . this year and all our years hereafter . . . we have but one job to do. A job for which we were made. A job for which a grateful nation slowly, purposefully, like water through a canyon, created us! Rooting out our enemies wherever they may hide, whatever mask they might wear. Find the enemy! Strike through the mask, men! Feel what is real within you and strike, men. I would fight the rising and setting of the sun if my nation called upon me to do so. This is our sacred duty, our bond as brothers, as soldiers. You know your positions, your task, your *purpose*. This, my men, my soldiers, my reality, this is why we do what we do. This day and always. Forever in eternity. Now let's execute!"

I draw out the *execute*, giving the word dual meaning in its delivery, and imagine a chorus of yells ringing out from the soldiers as they exclaim:

"Open the gates!"

"Hell yeah!"

"For Chemera!"

"For our nation!"

I raise the saber over my head, giving the raw steel a commanding flourish, and then sheathe the weapon with resounding purpose before reining my steed into a turning leap on her hind legs out the gates of the frontier fort and towards the supposed horde of enemies gathering in the distance, awaiting their fates.

We begin slowly weaving through the maze of dirt walls to get to the executive officer at the main gate. He's holding a small flashlight. His pants are un-bloused around untied boots. His brown undershirt his only top in the crisp morning air as he stands there, shoulders slumped, pretending he's not cold.

"Welp, here we go again. Have fun, sir," and the XO swings open the big metal outpost doors with a resounding clang against the mud wall and we begin our movement across the expanse. There is no horde awaiting us, only a stretch of desert highland floor and a short march to the village of Jacuz lying five kilometers to the east.

Silence.

The men fall in behind me, two by two, filing through the gate, the motivation they just demonstrated, at least in my head, tucked snugly away in their burdensome day packs as their heads and eyes slowly move to the desert floor knowing what is in store: an hour-long trudge across a wide open expanse to arrive at a village where they will be harassed by children for rations and candy. They will set up on a street corner, or on top of a building if they are lucky, and wait for something to happen, anything to happen—*a disruption* in time—while I speak to the locals about why we are here and how they can both help themselves and us at the same time:

". . . Oh, by the way, what can you tell me about the people on the border in Gaumela?"

". . . Oh, by the way, please stop aiding the insurgency by cowering in your village."

". . . Oh, by the way, we are not conquerors, we are liberators."

". . . Oh, by the way . . ."

This, dear reader, is what you have charged us to do. This is the way of our nation's foreign policy machinations. Whether you know this to be true or not.

I make the turn to the south with my radioman and interpreter. We move about fifty yards and stop to watch the still-darkened silhouettes of fighting men file out of the compound toward Jacuz. The men have good spacing. One of the silhouettes drops something, perhaps a hastily-grabbed MRE stuffed into a cargo pocket for the short walk, perhaps a box of ammo, and the accordion effect ubiquitous to all patrols begins. It only takes one. But when the platoon gets spread thin too early a few take a knee in the short halt. In thirty minutes time they will no longer take a knee unless told to specifically by a sergeant.

You should know that when the platoons are mounted in their armored vehicles, they tend to be a looser bunch, much harder to control and lacking in movement discipline. On foot the men dutifully march along and, except for a handful during a lengthy movement, can be counted on to maintain proper spacing and to exercise at least some modicum of infantry discipline. Sure, they will stop kneeling at some point, the non-kneelers multiplying in a ripple effect after the first soldier gets away with standing through the entire halt. The hope is that a sergeant will be there to fix the situation. But even sergeants get tired. Even sergeants are not that far removed from their own time as basic foot soldiers and will soon lose their commitment to discipline. There is a sweet spot for foot movements, usually between five and ten miles depending on the soldier's load, in which everyone involved in the movement can be counted on to do their duty and to police up the discipline of those who for whatever reason have a momentary lapse of judgment. Shorter than five miles and the men are in a rush to get to their objective, giving no time to the thought of being tired. Discipline comes naturally while the mission is fresh, when soldiers are still under the effect of orders. But as the approach march extends beyond five miles and starts pushing towards ten, you can watch the motivation and discipline drift away exponentially mile by mile. The twelve-mile march in training is a good exercise of internal leadership and enforcement of standards in which a unit can get the most bang for their training buck. Beyond twelve miles and you are just showing off, testing the men's minerals, and the juice is rarely worth the squeeze. A march beyond twelve miles and you would be well-advised to lighten the soldier's load, to quicken the soldier's pace in order to arrive at the objective still capable of mission execution. *Travel light, freeze at night.*

I will further contend that the behavioral differences exhibited whether soldiers are on foot or in a vehicle have to do with feelings of vulnerability and the human capacity for suffering, that when the men are buttoned up in heavily-armored trucks, they feel both powerful and resigned to fate, invincible yet completely vulnerable, a dualistic struggle between man and the mechanical beast he is forced to button up inside of and ride to his destiny. These dueling senses imbue them with a commanding concern for the mission at hand while simultaneously no longer caring what happens to them. In total control and yet possessing no control. A force suddenly vulnerable, at odds with their ability to project power. Fate holds the keys inside these giant armored vehicles, separating, insulating the soldier inside from the realities of the universe. The hole in the road, the innocuous pile of rubbish, the appearance of freshly overturned dirt, overwhelms and consumes, forcing the soldier within the hulking metal landcrawler to accept his life in this closed up behemoth as a roll of the dice, his destiny something he no longer controls and from which he cannot escape. He is a panicked, anxious, detached prophet in a great fish waiting and praying to be spit out onto the beach to do his work. The realization of his fate forces a mounted soldier to seek power any way he can, creating an ancient berserker caged within rolling armor, a mighty warrior seeking any way to regain the power that was taken from him the moment he found himself strapped inside this lurching, frothing, slogging hunk of metal and progress. He is a projection of power and identity honed over centuries of men going to war on horseback, of being both all-powerful and vulnerable at the same time, the deadly long spear developed solely for his demise, the rocket from his blind side employed for his express undoing in the blink of an eye. He is a great moving pedestal, a robotic cyclops that sees everything and nothing until the earth bursts forth and explodes beneath him, ending life as he knows it. By necessity he must care less for his own wellbeing. He is the unknown soldier going into combat wrapped in identity-robbing iron, aware of the vehicles to his left and right that he relies upon for protection but still locked inside himself, blocking out the complexity of life in exchange for the simple power dynamic afforded him inside a tank, a truck, an armored transport, a horse: kill now, because at any moment you will be killed.

The soldier on foot feels something different. He remains keenly aware with each and every laborious step that his very survival depends upon the abilities of the every-bit-as-exposed man to his left or right to look out for him. A monastic monist. His survival, his ability to do his duty, relies on the ability of the individual elements around him to create one living organism working in unison to control chaos, men around him he can look in the eye while facing an enemy he can also look in the eye. The soldier on foot knows how vulnerable he is, how wide open, how utterly alone. He cares too much for his own safety, becoming hyperaware of his surroundings, and only wants to make it to the next covered and concealed position should he fall prey to attack. The foot soldier is a cornered animal, skulking, crawling on hand and knee, pleading his way to the objective, ready to burst forth, exacerbating madness the moment madness bursts onto the stage. He sprays-and-prays, losing all sense of proportion to the situation. He charges that which announced its intent to end his life, bringing with him those to his left and right, forming a new beast, a mad group of crazed foot soldiers coalescing to form larger and larger groups as they seek protection for each other, the whites of each man's eyes exposed, identities carried deep inside their chests, seeking to destroy that which has interrupted the formation's concentration, that which has interrupted the air he freely breathes.

The mounted soldier is an empire unto himself, stomping through the land, destroying all he sees, lest he be destroyed by what he cannot see. The foot soldier is the peasant's revolt, attuned to the earth, feeling the beat of his own patriotic blood with each laborious step, watching, waiting to be pushed so that he may lash out in extremis. Both elements—mounted, dismounted—powerful, lethal. Both elements capable of invading, conquering, defeating, destroying any enemy that gets in their way. Each element vastly different, though, approaching their duty with a different mindset. Watching each of them work is an experience not for the faint of heart, and I well with intense pride watching my dismounts right now and yet still look forward to the next time we venture out in our trucks.

The men's helmets float and bob in the morning light as they make their way through the gate and into the world around them. Men on a mission. Culled from all walks of life, all backgrounds—my soldiers, your soldiers, our soldiers—come together in service for a concept we can never fully understand. The soldier knows nothing except that he must do something. It matters not what the cause is, for causes are beyond the soldier's ability to reason. Such men walk into the unknown as many times as necessary, a sacred duty to each other, a sacred duty to ideas bigger than themselves, bigger than you. They do not know why. Nor do they need to; their lives are lived in the present.

I lead my element south eight hundred meters into the smattering of small hills and rock outcroppings strewn across the highlands that constitute the beginnings of foothills leading to the great mountain ranges in the distance. This affords us the ability to provide overwatch for the other platoon and to react should they come under fire. At this range in a firefight, we would not be much help to the platoon, at best providing limited machine gun support with a large cone of fire. Sometimes, of course, just the sound of a machine gun on the flank is enough to make an enemy rethink their decisions. But we can interdict and support via other means as well—flank or assault an insurgent element, provide evacuation and medical support—in the event the exposed platoon came under fire. Any ambush Second Platoon encounters out in the open will likely come from these very rocky hills we occupy anyway, making our location advantageous to the fight.

You may immediately suspect, as others have posited, that the men walking in the open are *bait*, or *sitting ducks*, or *exposed targets*. Far from it. They are power projections. Power projections that make up part of the three distinct elements that best expand our presence. There is zero tactical sense in two platoons moving through the foothills in what would essentially end up being one element just asking to be ambushed, begging to get cut off from the other, inviting disaster. Second Platoon is in fact the main effort of the movement, their presence, bold and audacious across the open desert, a signifier of strength and courage. It is true, though, a fine line does exist between a sitting duck and a power projection.

Always twenty or so yards ahead of the main body, I am joined by my radioman as we act as our own scouts, the eyes and ears of our small element, observing everything around us and making decisions for the group. Across the flat open area in the wadi to the north, the first sergeant with the other half of First Platoon weave in and out of the dry riverbed, avoiding soft sand and main routes, traversing the micro-terrain, on the look-out for overturned dirt and strange piles of trash. They occasionally pop up three or four hundred yards in front of my section of men. I can barely make them out. If I did not know they were there, I might never see them. But I know. And once I see them, I cannot unsee them, becoming larger and clearer the more I focus in the light of the dawn. Once spotted, they make for inspiring images of our nation's warriors, clamoring over rocks, through small alleys and openings in the wadi network, their packs shifting as they move, the occasional glint of a piece of metal not properly subdued reflecting in the rising sun. Occasionally a soldier pops up onto a small bank and stands, hip-cocked, surveying the landscape, his weapon slung across his chest, his proud head on a swivel. He turns to lend a hand to the man behind him who climbs up on the outcropping and executes the same survey. One by one they act out this scene. Easy targets waiting to be cornered. The most patriotic poses are always the most tactically unsound.

My radioman and I take a knee behind a series of large rocks in demonstration of our own foot soldier discipline. We watch the movements of the other two elements and wait for the rest of our section to catch up. My radioman is both reliable and a good companion on missions. I chose him because he reminds me of myself as a young soldier: cocky but never taking himself too seriously. He too has adopted the *travel light, freeze at night* philosophy, so his burden is only about ten to twelve pounds more than mine with his radio and own spare batteries. He wears a single-ear headset under his helmet with push-to-talk button positioned on his chest. Clipped to the outside of his assault pack is a hand mic I can grab when I need to talk directly to someone or when I am directly summoned. He is especially adept at taking notes on a notepad he wears strapped to his right forearm, continuing to talk on the radio as he scribbles information down in even the nastiest of terrain or the ugliest of firefights. The kid is smart and good at his job, with a rugged, wiry look about him, a look that adds ten years to him and makes him appear as if he is always in need of a shave. He anticipates my needs and keeps me oriented to the situation. And he does not let his status as my right-hand man affect his relationship with the other soldiers on the compound. Everyone loves him. Most people respect basic competency when they see it.

The rest of the element catches up to us, being careful not to silhouette themselves, perhaps out of a conscious adherence to basic infantry skill and perhaps because they are putting on a show for their commander. I say nothing, scanning the open space and panning to look into the steep hills rising to our south that marks the natural terrain wall forming the border which we are tasked with being concerned.

I always assume I am being watched, a prudent assumption when you have invaded a country that resents your presence, taking mental notes of places where we might be ambushed if it were me hiding in the mountains doing the ambushing. Because if people from another nation invaded my nation for reasons I did not fully understand but some said was the result of a series of events that took place over many centuries which culminated in one cataclysmic event that I had no part in and all I wanted was to be left alone to tend to my chickens, and goats, and vegetables, and my family in a small mountain hovel, I cannot then imagine I would be one who would remain indifferent to this invasion. I suspect I would launch rockets at the invaders or attempt to ambush them when they were on the move to another village in hopes of *disrupting* their movement. Then I would go back to tending my chickens as if nothing ever happened. Even better in this formulation would be the existence of a border which I might use to my advantage.

Naturally, we want to avoid the places in which we could easily be ambushed. We want to mitigate as much as possible the chances that we are ambushed and, if we should come under attack, give ourselves the best chance of coming out of that attack unscathed. Sometimes these situations are unavoidable. There are only so many options presented in any one scenario. And route selection is a pain in the ass. Many times I am forced to look for places where we might be ambushed and where there is no getting around this particular route without significant pain and suffering and complete rerouting of the mission and then judge whether or not this location is a suitable place to face my death and to spend an eternity, as I have made up my mind that it would be better to spend an eternity in the place where I die in battle rather than be shipped back to our homeland, even if it is a homeland I love and cherish.

This idea, that my remains may stay in the place of my demise, makes me feel good. Our country, however, will most definitely return my remains to their point of origin despite my desire to be left where I lie. Our country's custom of returning fallen soldiers to their home of record is to be honored, yes. But I do believe there is validity to my own thoughts on the matter.

Death and the ensuing afterlife will ring much truer if the physical body is allowed to remain in place, fertilizing the battleground that future warriors will undoubtedly tread. To die in a struggle for power only to be returned to the safety of our homeland is a noble but flawed idea. If our nation insists on returning me to my point of origin, perhaps I did not belong here to begin with. So I look for ambush sights and evaluate their potential as final resting places. A false comfort but a comfort nonetheless. We are all returned to our nation of origin, dead or alive, remembered or forgotten. I know these thoughts are not conducive to good leadership—they are defeatist—and I keep them to myself, only telling you now because you might like to know my thoughts on the matter and how these thoughts inform my current philosophy. These ideas are better left to my more pensive moments when I am alone during my evening constitutionals around Chemera, not in the middle of a patrol.

The First Platoon element, led by a competent lieutenant and accompanied by the first sergeant in the northern wadi system, occasionally disappears entirely then pops out of the expansive dry river bed as my section weaves in and out of the rocky hills avoiding the well-trod paths and goat trails found throughout the terrain. Now all three elements are beginning their convergence on the town of Jacuz. The village grows in our collective sight as we make our approach from our own individual viewpoints. I see an angle, an opening between buildings that my radioman does not. The squad leader halfway back of our formation approaches just ten meters to the left of us, reaches this same distance from the village as me and my radioman only two minutes later, and yet he sees and smells a completely different village. The first sergeant hones in on an opening, an ingress and egress route, from an opposite line in our three-element formation. A private, lugging the M240 machine gun across the high desert floor, focuses on a chicken that dashes across the main entry to the village and wonders what has upset the chicken so much. All one element, completely different perspectives on this one objective that is only just now beginning to wake up, only just now facing the day as their conquerors approach.

We must first kill an hour in an extended long halt just outside the town: observing the people move about, feeling the morning inhales and exhales of their existence as a village. The argument is made that this technique allows any insurgents in the village to escape or to hide their bombs and weapons before we move into town. But they know we are coming. They have known since the sun came up that we were on our way. They have always known we were on our way. There is no element of surprise with our nation's army. You know what we are doing even if those of us inside of the army do not. And, anyway, this is not a targeted hit, we are here to win these people over to our side, their hearts and minds, to convince these people that our way of life is better than theirs. But I fear the loyalty of these people runs deep, loyalty to a concept none of us truly understand. As does mine. As does yours, I am sure. But we will conquer this town, Jacuz, on our terms and by our own definition. For today, anyway.

6.

0730. THE SWEAT ON our backs begins to cool, and I know it is time to get to work. I grab the hand mic and give the word for Second Platoon to launch to their positions on the outskirts of the village as First Platoon pushes further in to form an inner cordon.

Still quite early but I am sick of waiting. The small number of young village vagabonds we do meet at this time of morning represent only a fraction of what will stream through our formations and security positions throughout the day. The littlest ones, out and about since the crack of dawn, peek around corners and through the large metal doors of their family's mud-walled compound, excited at the prospect of treats today. They know the rhythms of our nation's patrols. A half-naked toddler moves between buildings to no one's concern. A handful of women, three or four dark entrancing beauties, fetch water from a village well, their heads and faces covered. Occasionally a veil or head covering will slip during the conduct of these female chores and I catch a glimpse of their determined faces. In many a weak moment, I convince myself that when a headscarf slips off it is for my benefit, and I fantasize about starting a family with two or three of them, hidden away forever in a discrete mud-walled compound of my own, my mountain palace, like an ancient general who came to conquer a kingdom but found something far more compelling between the thighs of the exotic and the unknown. The fight to prevent these thoughts from taking control is vicious and continuous.

I task my platoon leaders, both motivated young officers with stars in their eyes, to work their areas as best they can by interacting with the locals and gathering intelligence. I will summon them along with the platoon sergeants to my own position around *1030* so that we can exchange information, synthesize our own thoughts, and send the info higher before pushing the leaders back out to their positions to wait for the movement back to Chemera in time for hot evening chow.

The men are looser out on patrol, like teenagers recently released from the grips of a harsh religious upbringing, more willing to share jokes, gossip, talk about the locals, than they are in the constricting confines of Outpost Chemera, a state of affairs I chalk up to both the amount and type of action we have seen since arriving in country and the nature of our quaint existence in the wide open highlands as easy targets for those who, for whatever reason, wish us to leave their country or die in their country.

In our eight months here, while outside Outpost Chemera and on patrol, we have seen two dynamically coordinated ambushes, came under hit-and-run ambushes three times, became decisively engaged with a mounted insurgent element three times, and conducted two raids in which we just missed our targeted combatant on both occasions but were still able to detain known associates.

The previous report may also be rendered by saying that in our eight months here we have been ambushed twice by a few men hiding behind boulders in the foothills, had a few local farmers fire one or two potshots at us as we left an area on patrol, actually identified and engaged a pick-up truck with insurgents that shot at us then drove off, and conducted two raids at night in which the targets—likely men whose cell phone conversation with an uncle or cousin across the border was misinterpreted and poorly analyzed by our intelligence assets because that is what experts do, analyze data to fit their prescribed narrative—were long gone but we still went ahead and arrested a few of his cousins and sent them back to the bigger Forward Operating Base Palermo anyway.

These are two versions of the same report. My own relationship to these two reports fluctuates based on my current state of loyalty and sense of duty as a soldier who fights where he is told and wins where he fights.

Report one: *I'm getting after it and taking it to the enemy. Really disrupting and having good effects, sir.*

Report two: *I'm wasting my time milling about these mountain foothills waiting for tragedy to strike in a war that we have waged for many years, sir.*

Most of us have been in combat before save for the lowest of enlisted men and the fresh-faced lieutenants. This is, however, the quietest deployment most of us have experienced. At least this is what we tell ourselves when we jaw-jack about everything and nothing while out on patrol waiting for time to pass so we can head back to Chemera for dinner. The power we once wielded has begun to stagnate, to seek more fruitful ground. The feeling of most is that it might be time to live off the stories of the past, a time when our power was never in question, when rockets landed with effect, when ambushes meant the earth would soon explode all around and beneath us, and we were allowed to go on the offensive with impunity to maintain our death grip on the power bestowed upon us by our affiliation with our nation's army.

It might also be said that both versions of reports of our experience here during this particular deployment depend on your own experience level, faculties of perception, and ability to process various trauma. Normality to some represents severe abnormalities to others. Or we might say sensitivity is as sensitivity feels, and everyone can hide behind what they profess to feel about a situation, a report, or the nature of their personal experiences.

You already know I do not typically read military books and studies—at least not those that purport to be non-fiction—so I am not even sure where I might have run across the statistic I am about to provide you. I read books about whaling, ancient loves, and poetry. Why drown in our own watered-down glories when we have been given so much to pursue, so much sunlight in which to swim? But what I have learned is that in previous wars the soldiers of my nation died from their wounds at a rate four times that of my generation's war, which leads me to believe that advances in medical care and the ability to rapidly evacuate the wounded via helicopter extractions across most of the country account for what would be my war's lower killed-in-action rate when compared to previous wars. Let it be known that my generation's war produces a lot of soldiers who suddenly find themselves without arms or legs or are otherwise disfigured. Let this fact speak for itself and adjust your analysis accordingly.

Regardless of how you read these reports or how I present said reports, there is no denying that the bulk of our combat experience on this deployment consists of the twice-weekly absorption of rockets from the mountains to the south of Chermera that we suspect are being launched directly from the border village of Gaumela and that absorbing incoming rockets twice a week does a number on the nerves, particularly when you cannot see the enemy and he has likely been to the compound several times on any number of errands, from contract work to cooking for the local border police to socializing at a festive dance party. So while I have seen much more action in previous adventures into this foreign land, kicked in many more doors at midnight, assaulted objectives over entire weeks, to sit here statically and just accept these rocket salvos as part of my duty is a tough pill to swallow. At some point someone will be killed by one of these rocket attacks and we will either be told to leave Chemera or be given permission to move into Gaumela for a clearing operation. More likely, should such an event take place, the order to abandon Chemera will come down and the unfortunate soul whose death served as the catalyst for the order to move can rest easy knowing his sacrifice prompted our military leaders to second guess the position of this outpost five kilometers from an international border between a country engaged in a war and a country pretending to not be at war. At this point, though, having avoided any major catastrophes in the eight months of our deployment so far, the men have lost the desire to go kicking what we believe to be a hornet's nest. At month eight of a twelve-month deployment, it is typically time to check the box on your five to seven patrols a week and call it a tour. The only exceptions to this way of thinking are the platoon leaders on their first combat tours. Lieutenants never change. Neither do most privates, sergeants, first sergeants, sergeants major, captains, majors, colonels, or generals. I do not know, dear reader, if you have ever changed. But we must remain pliable in our thoughts and open to the opportunity, open to receiving change, open to renewal when our perceptions are shaken and new realities are presented. Nevertheless, I still know that few of us will ever actually embrace and accept these new perceptions of the world that are sometimes gifted to us.

Positioning myself in the center of Jacuz, I wait patiently for the village elders to make their way to me, as they invariably will. For this mission, as for all others, I have made an elaborate plan with phase lines, blocking positions, screen lines, tasks and purposes for each subordinate element, redundancies in communication methods, alternate routes, all the things that make up a good operations order. This has become second nature to me. Each team leader, the lowest level of leader required to attend my company operations order, understands his purpose and is further required to provide clear and concise brief-backs to demonstrate that he does indeed understand the patrol, that he is fully oriented to the situation and can take decisive action based on the end state relative to his task and what he observes on the ground. They will then go on the mission and do whatever they want as if they have never even heard of such a thing as an operations order. When questioned, they will contend either that they are in fact in the right place doing the right thing or that they never really understood the guidance to begin with.

So why concern myself with the details? Most of my peers, even my bosses, issue bare-bones plans that only go so far as their ability to maneuver little scraps of paper around on a terrain model or manipulate icons on a computer slide presentation. They create vague, nonsensical plans based on no sense of terrain, no analysis of the enemy's thoughts and capabilities, and no consideration as to the precise application of individual firepower and the triangulation of warfare. If pressed for more information, these staff officers will preach what has come to be known as a *concept of the operation*, which is nothing more than tiny informational slivers of a mission, mere whiffs of a full-blown operation handed down from their predecessors and which they themselves cannot clearly articulate. Or the question will be addressed by the smoke-and-mirrors trick of calling the answer *nebulous* or *transparent*. What they really mean is *opaque*, but this is beside the point. The briefer then deflects the question and shifts the topic towards some logistical issue or an administrative point completely unrelated to the tactical situation or the operational needs of the mission or, if the briefer is really insecure, he will attack the questioner either directly or with a passive-aggressive attack couched in humor.

In the end, whether my plans are ever executed to their exact specification is of little concern to me. My idealism was long ago checked at the gates of military bureaucracy and mediocrity. Maybe this is something my superiors latched onto many years ago, and they are the better soldiers for it.

Perhaps. But even if my plans are not executed exactly as envisioned in my head, and even if my bosses consider me a smug troubleshooter or even an overthinker who misses the larger point of the operation, I am not convinced this is a colossal failure on my part or on the part of my men nor even necessarily an entirely bad situation. I need the planning time. So long as duty to the mission is served, so long as the labor required of me as an officer is complete, particularly in matters of life and death, then I can sleep with a clear conscious. What my subordinates do with the information is beyond my control. Here it is. Now *disrupt*.

The sun makes quick work of any morning coolness as my small security detail and I—my radioman, an artillery lieutenant and his NCO, and a three-man fire team culled from one of the squads—begin to establish ourselves in the center of the village. The length of the main thoroughfare through town runs east-west and has the customary array of tiny storefronts selling assorted goods and services—a motorcycle repair shop, a tiny shop with everything from chips and cold drinks to hair dye, a storefront full of animal feed and fertilizer—as well as a few walled-off gardens and orchards and several homes. These homes, like all the homes in this country, are constructed with two large, heavily decorated metals doors providing the only color in the walled-in mud-constructed compounds. From this center point, the rest of the village expands in an elaborate maze of narrow roads and even narrower alleys, compound after compound, with the occasional storefront the lone interruption to the labyrinth of private dwellings.

I envision these villages and their functionality as akin to the relationships found in my book about whaling, a book I have read before but, like so many other things in my life, whose meaning, insomuch as I derive any meaning and understanding from the text, has shifted in my post-combat life. Many books that are touted as classics in our country become either completely useless to me after my combat experiences or take on new meaning. A rereading of these books following my forays into combat brings with it a new comprehension I now recognize to be their true light in respect to my own light, though I know this understanding also to be fleeting and only relevant to my emotional state at the time. But this renewed light helps me to deal with my own newfound realities and subsequently assists in developing beneficial psychological tactics and strategies upon my return to foreign soil to do our nation's bidding. I am provided new coping mechanisms heretofore unknown to me but for which I am grateful. There are many such coping mechanisms we soldiers rely upon in our post-combat lives, and each brings a new sense of being to the present.

Some of these classics of my nation's literary canon do in fact make the soldier's experience their subject and, while I do not normally read such books, I have on occasion found myself longing to be the type of person who enjoys tales of combat and the soldier experience, such as it is, and so I gave these books, books that were forced upon me first during my formative educational years, a second chance. When I first read these books as a younger man, the books only served to arouse in me a sense of obligation to the plight of the soldier and the struggles he endures. I possessed no point of reference for that struggle, and so this newly aroused sense of obligation could only turn to pity for the soldier. I can, with what I believe to be authority, proclaim that the last thing a soldier wants is your pity. Pity and victimization is an attitude reserved for the weak. A soldier wants respect and acknowledgment for the differences he perceives to be within him. To hell with pity. Since you trusted him to execute foreign policy in your name, he believes you must also trust his voice later when he begins to see the world through new eyes even if that view is suddenly at odds with the creation you laid out for him and worked so hard to instill.

As you can see, then, our perceptions, both yours and mine, can change. But nothing else. Just as the way a soldier, when he returns to our nation after a combat tour, approaches traffic congestion, enters a room, rounds street corners, and responds to loud noises differently due to these new perceptions, the way I come to understand or to not understand the classics of our nation's literary canon changes. But do not pity these changes. Acknowledge them. Acknowledge them so we can be left alone to tend to the chickens on our small mountain farms, working together to once again serve each other in the understanding that no man is an island unto himself but rather a patchwork of former selves held together by a fraternal spirit of a much-longed-for separation and isolation, a cult of silence and solitude working towards a common good.

This, as you may have already guessed, accounts for the way the men in the whaling book I am reading—and perhaps this is a book you have read or are at least familiar with, as it is considered essential reading in understanding the machinations of our nation's shared culture—have changed for me personally in my pre-combat and post-combat reading. These sailors share much of themselves with each other. They overlap one another. They lose themselves in one another in pursuit of a great beast. They are one. Yet somehow these whaling men still manage to carve out a space of their own, their own unique identities, amongst the monotonous repetition of day-to-day life. In their pursuit of the enemy each man finds himself under great and extraordinary difficulties, yet they come together in an effort to pursue and kill their prey. Each man has a job to do. A purpose to their life.

The men on the whaling ship may warrant individual, unique descriptions in the pages of the book, yet when these pages are put together and read, they create a wholeness that propels the ship's operations and ensures accomplishment of the mission at the behest of a vengeful captain. The villages in which I currently find myself in, Jacuz included, are no different: no rules or regulations, no directives from experts, just a mosaic held firmly together by a historic tradition rooted in fighting those who would conquer and change their way of life. *All hands on deck.* There is a great and mighty beast to defeat. You cannot *disrupt* that which defies disruption, that which is indifferent to your power.

Most of the soldiers in my company hate these villages, cannot understand how they function or why anyone would live like this.

"You know why third-world countries are third world? Because they're inhabited by people from the third world," my soldiers say.

"How many of these people does it take to change a light bulb? What the fuck is a light bulb?" they joke.

But I feel most at home when surrounded by the comforting mud walls and the melding of one building into another which serves to create a patchwork of places, all separate yet interconnected by a common sense of themselves as a people. I miss our homeland, sure. Believe me when I say this. But I find our home, our nation, does not operate like the whaling ship I read about when I am left all alone in the nest that is my commander's quarters or when on patrol in these small villages in this land we have occupied.

The town of Jacuz, of course, does not change its disposition upon our arrival. It never does. The village maintains the exact same rhythm and pace it has for millennia, seeing no reason to change its habits simply because another invader has arrived in an attempt to change its essence. And why else would anyone come from another world to occupy their world unless they sought to change something deep within their core? For the people of Jacuz, it is just easier to continue to do what they do rather than bend to the short-sighted whims of invaders. They will win out. They always have. *We will not be disrupted.*

I am told that there are many rumors among the locals, told to me by my interpreters, about why the locals believe us to be in their country, about some great wrong that has been carried out against us in our homeland and for which we arrived to exact retribution. But these are just rumors among woman and shepherds and carry no weight with the local elders. To the elders, what we want is power, just like everyone else who has endeavored to invade their lands. Neither of us really understands what the other believes and neither of us believes what we know the other to understand. Every faction thinks the other faction is wrong. The sentiment may make more sense to me now having spent a large portion of my adult life trying to make heads or tails of these local rumors and the rumors that circulate within the world of my nation's foreign policy creators.

Establishing myself in the center of the village, I point to a lone fruit tree in the center of the lot with patches of grass splayed around it like prostrate worshippers.

"This is *our* tree," I say, directing my entourage to set up shop while the rest of the element peels off to secure the four corners of the roughly five-hundred-meter square lot, "This is where we belong."

I make two slow, meandering laps, holding my head high and on a swivel, inspecting each position and vantage point, every nook and cranny and alleyway that empties into the lot before I move to the newly dubbed operations center at the base of our tree. Such displays of occupation are necessary to the proceedings. The occupier of a village, whether the first visit or one of a thousand visits stretched out over many years, should arrive in full control without a hint of timidity. We have a job to do. We will stand center-point, alone and unafraid, basking in the exposure of vacant fields. A sniper can easily take me out with one shot, a risk well worth the theatrical effect, a risk that is mine and mine alone, a bit of drama added to a monotonous, droning play of limitless acts.

Hugging this small tree, its yellow-green fruit just beginning to fill out the rubbery branches, my small contingent sets up their maps and tracking boards and portable antennas from which we can communicate better with the battalion staff farther away at Palermo. The movement to Jacuz has taken a little more than ninety minutes, a quick move and occupation, and I feel a little out of sorts. This feeling is only exacerbated by the appearance of three village elders already making their way to my position.

0758. Highly unusual for elders to make an appearance in these villages at this hour rather than the younger men attending to typical chores and work duties. There are only a few elders showing up now, on the younger side of the village elder scale, probably new to their positions and eager to start discussions. But getting settled in position, gathering a sense of the moment and the terrain, and sending reports to Higher are my priorities right now. The conversational game can wait till mid-morning. Now is not the time to be bombarded by elders. But the appearance of these three this early means many more are on the way. All signs point to a long day of grievances and arguments with people looking for answers and asking for more respect from the invaders. They do not *really* know why we are here. Cannot fully understand. Nor do they *really* believe anything we say. Any reasoned argument or call for change will be met with the same excuses, blame, and justifications. Much to their credit, though, they will feed us, at least me and my entourage, and keep us supplied with tea. These people resent our presence, are indifferent to any reasoning behind our mission, care even less for the border than the people of Gaumela, but we will not go without tea and a meal.

"Come on, man. Are you kidding me?" I yell at the security team just getting established at their intersection.

The first sergeant rounds an opposite corner and moves quickly toward the elders to see the situation resolved.

"I got this, sir!"

He is in the zone. This is the first sergeant's bread and butter, his part of the patrol to shine: initial security and defense. He dutifully checks on positions, makes the rounds to as many of his soldiers as he can, makes sure the company perimeter is established, defensive positions properly manned and provisioned, and then finds a nice comforting tree in a shady orchard to relax under while he directs all villagers my way. Well played. He is young for a first sergeant, fast-tracking through the enlisted ranks, not in shape but not really out of shape either. He's just there, or here. More importantly, he understands his historic role in the proceedings and accomplishes his mission with the unquestioning gusto exhibited by a dedicated company man. I am happy to let him run around and make sure security is set and then let him recover for the day. These little actions, this attention to detail he thrives on, brings everyone back to the same level. Enforce exacting patrol standards. Ensure each soldier does exactly what they are put on this earth to do. Ensure the pieces are in place and reconnoitered for medevac should the need arise. Test the redundancy of communications between elements. Make the ship sail. Bolster the unity of effort required to speed the craft through the crashing waves all around, a model of efficiency cutting through the chop with ease. Of course he cannot, nor is he expected to, visit each and every defensive position of a two-platoon element in a village this size, but he is able to bounce around to more than a few. So long as the men see him on these patrols and know that if he does not visit them this patrol, he will definitely check on them the next patrol, then he has done his job. This is an infantry company at work. And today, we are barely out of the harbor.

7.

NOTHING HAS CHANGED IN Jacuz since we last visited. The same trash blows in the street as it did a month and half before, as it did six months prior, as it did two years before, and a hundred years before that. Not unlike that faded, empty bag of chips you see two or three days in a row on a daily jog in our own nation until one day you do not notice the trash anymore and you are unsure whether or not the refuse was picked up, if the trash just blew away, or if you have just become so inured to the presence of little bits of litter on your path that you no longer take conscious notice of the invasion on your environment. Then suddenly the trash reappears and you are again unsure if it is the same trash or a new piece of litter, maybe it's a soda bottle this time, and you cannot remember whether or not the piece of trash that was first brought to your attention was a soda bottle or was it something else entirely that has once again turned up on your jogging path, and you are reassured by this new presence because whether or not it's the same piece of trash or not matters little; what matters is that the trash is always there to see and was likely always there. To complain about. To not fix. The comfort of sameness allows you to keep jogging just as the sameness of this village allows me to do my work here.

A patina coats these villages, like antique furniture, worn with the natural ravages of time: solid, reliable, real, and stable. Unmovable. As if anything can happen here today and it would not change one thing about the village or the war. The company of infantrymen that just happens to have arrived this day, a small fraction of the thousands of soldiers that have trod this ground before, could go on a brutal killing spree, rounding up as many men, woman, and children in this village as they can, stack them up in the center of the village, set the bodies ablaze, and not a single tenet, goal, or end state would change in our army's mission. A ruthless, barbarous act that I am sorry I even presented to you in this example, but an act that would nevertheless be written off as the actions of a rogue commander and his men. This heinous act would be disavowed. We would be properly punished for our horrid crimes. Some form of restitution would be provided the survivors of such an inhuman act. But our army would remain, assuring the locals that this was not the policy of our great nation and that those responsible for these heinous acts would pay for such actions.

Likewise, a thousand insurgents could come streaming in from the mountains to behead each and every one of us, leave us to bleed our dirty foreign blood in the streets of Jacuz, and still there would be no change. The army of our nation, a nation I love dearly, would denounce such acts as the desperate acts of animalistic and deranged terrorists, insurgents, and criminal syndicates with no hope of winning our justified war of liberation. Our army would then go right back to outlandish outpost placement, the weighing down of soldiers with lasers and radios and more personal protective equipment than a medieval knight, and to bickering for years over the formatting of patrol schedule spreadsheets and supply request forms sent through a network of bureaucratic channels. No matter what could happen, no matter what does happen, the circle will be unbroken, the village unchanged, the same trash blowing in the wind.

With the early arrival of the elders at bay I finish my first reports and set about checking on platoon leaders and clearing them to do some easy reconnaissance in and around their sectors. This is as much for their own training as anything else. They will interview a few adult age males as they see fit, inspect a few homes, and spend some time among the locals. Let the people get used to our presence, introduce the act of soldiers entering their homes and invading their space as a justified part of their existence, a new normal, such as it is, such as it ever will be.

The fresh lieutenants love this exercise, not yet fully aware that this merely constitutes a small part of their officer development, checking the box of their loyalty training, providing them a small taste of the power they each crave. They are to get just a whiff of what is in store, propelling them ever upward to seek more power as they move up the chain of command during their careers. These are young patriots with promotions, stars, in their eyes. Maybe they will stumble upon a great find, a high-value target who slips up and lets himself be caught. But more often than not they walk away from these taskings with a firmer grasp of the culture and the territory in which an infantry soldier fights, better armed for the day when they too will possess increasing levels of responsibility as commanders of our nation's military forces. The more time a soldier spends among the people, the better developed his sense of the terrain, both human and geographic, will become, the more adept he will become in overpowering the populace.

Once the platoon leaders meet with me at our central tree, we will discuss what they saw, compartmentalize the information as best we can, and tie this low-level intelligence into our assessment of the village together with what comes out of the ensuing meeting with the elders. These are all processes the battalion intel staff should utilize to paint a larger picture for the commander, though most of the time the S2 never uses any of the information we provide, preferring to base their analysis on what they think the bosses want to hear, an odd utilization of their own power to influence, a group of sycophants in service to ideas rather than truth.

Since we arrived earlier than usual the platoon leaders are anxious and prepared to confer by *1000*, and after the ubiquitous railing against the system, the old sports stories, and less talk about women than you might think, I send them back out to their respective positions by *1100* to wait for *the word* that tells them my own meeting with the elders is over and we are free to return to our base of operations at Chemera, return to our burn pit and lukewarm showers and comic book movies and pornography. The elders however, are visibly anxious today, having already reconvened around our security perimeter. The arrival of tea and cakes from a bevy of teen boys is the final straw, and I welcome the elders by taking off my helmet, handing my rifle to my radioman, and lighting a cigarette.

I quite enjoy these discussions with the village elders. We all know they are useless; even the old men who sit and fondle their beads and stroke their beards and stare at me intently know these meetings are useless. They have seen all this before. But I feel like the elders appreciate my upfront admittance that most of the things they have been promised over the many years of our invasion will never happen. You may find this odd, maybe even subversive to my mission. But I call it respect for my fellow man. They are never upset when I tell them this. They always knew these were empty promises never to be delivered. The projects or products promised bear no weight on how this village functions. They laugh at our nation's misplaced priorities and misunderstanding of their own needs and wants. The hubris of others can be a form of entertainment if one remains detached and indifferent.

"A new water well? Sure, we'll take it if you want to waste your time and money building one. But we have been here for hundreds of years, with water, and we will continue to be here for hundreds of years, with water."

"New rugs for our places of worship? Sure, we'll take them if you want to waste your time and money passing them out. But we have rugs. And we will continue to have rugs. And just because you give us a few cheaply made rugs does not mean we will suddenly become loyal to you, the invaders that have, in our concept of time, only been here a short while, a matter of minutes, but in your concept of time have been here for countless years."

I assure them that our unkept promises are not out of belligerence or any sort of malice towards them but rather a result of inefficiencies in our system, arrogance, and our nation's tendency to favor naive optimism over pragmatism, money over hard truths. It is hard to convince them of this, however, when they see aircraft fly over, know we spy on them with drones, know we can see them at night, know we have computers at Chemera that speak to each other around the globe. It is hard for them to believe a country with so much cannot build a village water pump after promising a pump for many years, whether the people here need one or not. The fact remains that some overzealous go-getter before me told them our nation would provide them one. So no, they do not really care about a new well or water pump or backpacks for schoolkids or soccer balls. Instead, they simply marvel at our fabrications, our lies, and our inability to come through on our word. All I do is tell them I will not make any promises. I cannot account for what others have told them. Nor do I care. Some elders understand and shake their heads in agreement, some do so with a smile. Most of these men are more keenly aware of the way our nation works, and does not work, than most of my peers.

There exists a genuine feeling of hospitality in these meetings. A hospitality that borders on the suspicious. Then two elders will get into an argument, demonstrating the same small-town feuds that crop up in our own country's village councils. Of course, here in Jacuz these feuds go back several hundred years, and I am somehow expected to overcome these century-old fights to which I am not privy nor have any backstory in order to get information that might be useful in my disruption mission. I have been instructed to try and make these village squabbles work to my advantage, to pit one neighbor against another for a piece of intelligence. But information garnered in this way is rarely reliable. Better to stay out of their business and just do my job the best I can.

There is something different in this meeting, though, a real sense of brewing discord just under the surface of our so far trite discussion. The group of village elders finally gets down to business by turning the conversation over to the elder who has consistently presented himself as the one in charge. He does not seem particularly aligned with the group of young elders and he is definitely not in the group of older elders who fidget with their beads and are here simply out of respect for their earthly longevity. He is caught in the middle of the village elder demographic and carries himself with a quiet dignity I immediately respect. We have not met before, which I find strange. Probably a local shop owner. Probably has a decent size herd of goats. Probably a busy man.

The group goes silent and focuses on this elder as he moves to the front of our semi-circled gathering, his dark, brooding features glued to my gaze. He picks a couple pears from our tree. Two birds, disturbed by his fruit picking, scream and squawk, disturbing the silence. He hands one of the pieces of hard fruit to me, gestures for me to *take, eat,* and looks me square in the eyes as he bites into the flesh without a word, never losing eye contact.

I bite into the hard, not-fully-ripe flesh, the fruit already hot in the morning sun. I taste the young pear on the back of my tongue, the sharp tang darting up and across my cheekbones. I try not to show discomfort with the experience.

He is ready to talk. I instruct my interpreter to translate each and every word as close to verbatim as he can, word for word, no interpretations, direct translation.

The interpreter begins:

"The last time your men were here, some children saw them using the bathroom in a well. How do you say, sir . . . pissing? When the soldiers saw that the children saw them, they chased them and they are catching two of them and slapping them across the face and yelling at them. We are very concerned about this and want to know what you are going to do?"

I feel as if every eye in this circle is boring a hole right through me. I am a little dismayed, though by no means shocked. My interpreter adds:

"This is very bad, sir."

"You think? Thanks. I fucking know it's bad."

"Yes, sir. He wants to know what you are going to do?"

"I heard you the first time."

I turn and throw the half-eaten pear into the alley, look down at my boots for a moment, then return the unwavering gaze of this elder.

Caught off guard for the first time in many years, I stare back intently at this man not more than ten years my elder. Had a man wearing a suicide vest stepped into the village square I would have had a clearer idea of what actions to take. But I am unprepared for this scenario in which I have no frame of reference, no historic starting point from which to launch. The tools I need to deal with this may be deep inside me somewhere but have been tucked away far too long and are not readily available. I am, however, familiar with this sensation of being lost in the moment, of feeling out of time. It is the same feeling of being completely lost in myself while back home in our own country and forced to suddenly deal with a situation in which the participants, the actions, and the reactions are unexpected and foreign. A change takes place within my deepest psyche, a change is taking place even now, a change as a matter of survival.

"I have absolutely no idea what I will do."

8.

You should at this point be provided some sense of how life plays out for me outside of my call to service in perpetual warfare. It may be helpful to my plight, such as it is, if you understand these events that cause internal conflicts to flare up whenever I am faced with uncertainty in situations that do not involve actual combat, much like the one in which I currently find myself.

Armed with this knowledge, dear reader, you might better understand the ways in which two worlds can collide, though there is naturally some degree of uncertainty as to whether or not there is any correlation between the way I feel now, in this moment, having been told my soldiers pissed in a village well, and the way I feel in moments of uncertainty back in our homeland. But I want you to know the truth, such as it is. These are all coping mechanisms that make up who we are in relation to who we once were.

I believe these issues to be outside my control, just as the triggering events are outside my control, and just as the machines that have put into place various palliatives designed to ensure I remain a fully functioning soldier in a volunteer system are out of my control. And just as the mechanisms within a watch can never truly know the time, the soldiers inside a war zone can never fully comprehend the workings of the machine to which they are a critical component, never fully understanding how time moves differently in our nation when one is fighting an insurgency just five kilometers from an internationally recognized border. Yet they must still do their job without fail. To question your purpose and role in the machine truly marks the beginning of failure.

One of the many cogs designed to assist the machine in its smooth operation is a *by-unit rotational mechanism* in which entire groups of soldiers are ferried back and forth across vast oceans, generally for a year at a time, in order to project our military might and to do what the machine does best via the dynamic application of our nation's foreign policy directives. Groups of soldiers arrive en masse to a designated war zone in order to replace another group of soldiers who have been in the war zone for roughly a year, and the cycle continues in perpetuity until our great nation loses interest in this particular projection of power and focuses its formidable might elsewhere.

I do not know with complete certainly why this *by-unit rotational system* exists. I should not even be asking such questions. But here I am, now bearing this truth, in the hopes of justifying my actions to you. So if I were to venture a guess, this *by-unit rotational system* likely exists as an empathetic desire to maintain the psychological wellbeing of an all-volunteer service and to provide at least the semblance of both military unit cohesion and a personal family support structure in the life of a soldier.

But I will let you know that I believe when one is sent on a mission to enforce their nation's foreign policy, it is best to maintain this force projection until the task is finished. In fact, early in my military career I assumed this was the policy of our nation's army, as I was not allowed to return home following an event as simple as a day at the machine gun range or extended field training exercises until that training mission was done, my weapon was cleaned and stowed, and all my gear was accounted for and inventoried. Further, no one in the unit with which I was training would be allowed to go home, or to return to the barracks, or to see their families, until everyone in the unit had returned from the range or other training exercise. What we started together, we finished together. I always assumed this was baseline training designed to establish a foundation for the disposition our nation's army would assume when we embarked once again on combat operations during my generation's carrying of the endless torch of warfare our nation has decided is a necessity in the modern world. The lesson was clear: you do not return home to your creature comforts nor to your loved ones until we can all safely and rightly say *mission accomplished.*

Under this *by-unit rotational system* we will find that in any given three-to-five-year period, a soldier like myself will suddenly be thrust back into the safety of the lush mountains, forests, and creeks of his boyhood, back to the small towns and villages from which the vast majority of our nation's soldier's hail, for two to three years at a time. We will find ourselves once again wandering through the tangled memories of our pre-combat life attempting to recreate a once pastoral life in our homeland that has eluded us since the day we were first compelled to take up arms against those designated by our nation's leaders as enemies. The machine thinks it is giving us a break, a well-needed respite from the rigors of war. Perhaps there is more to this than I, a mere cog in the machine, can see. But for me this break only makes one long for one side or the other. A life split and divided against itself, forced to straddle lines of demilitarization, rules of engagement, the law of land warfare, and the mountains and creeks and forests that make up all the various boundaries in our pre-combat civilian life cannot function in any healthful way. Insurgencies arise in such situations.

Granted, much of the time back in the homeland is spent in continued training at various rifle ranges, situational training exercises, and in multi-week extended field exercises in preparation for our next rotation to war so as to prevent any degradation in combat skills. Still, a soldier is afforded a considerable amount of personal time to do with what they want while back in our nation.

This redeployment to the homeland for extended periods of time while awaiting my turn to once again enforce our nation's foreign policy naturally involves venturing out to mingle with a variety of civilians of various stripes and upbringings, all of whom possess a diverse range of societal and cultural training. I mean no disrespect, reader, if any of the situations I provide here as examples of my struggles in our nation ring true for you. We are on different sides of the fence, and yet these interactions become part and parcel of our shared lives as citizens of a free nation we both must love dearly. It is in these interactions with my fellow citizens, the people that make up the freedom-loving populace of our nation, that my *Civilians in Homeland Reaction and Interaction Syndrome Transfiguration*—or CHRIST—manifests itself in my life.

My CHRIST acts as a necessary balm, a healing ointment, a lubricant if you will, between my role as a servant to this nation and the interaction I have with the civilians who send me to do their bidding based on policy and prescribed foreign policy directives. My CHRIST may strike at any moment, and the actions of my CHRIST serve to reconcile my place in the world while acting as a steady guide in suppressing the original habits placed within me upon my creation as a soldier. And there is nothing I can do to resist this transfiguration. The only way in which to prepare myself for CHRIST is to remain receptive to the working of the syndrome within me. In this manner, I hope to grow and better understand the true nature of what is taking place deep within my psyche.

This CHRIST works in mysterious ways. One way for you to understand this phenomenon may come by way of my interactions with motor vehicles. Without a doubt, upon coming back from a year-long bout of combat, I am much more hesitant on the roads, steering clear as much as possible of suspicious vehicles and road oddities: the tailgating oversized and lifted pick-up truck, small piles of trash dropped on the side of the road for some inexplicable reason, the deep bass that fills the air, vibrates my entire car, exploding all around me out of what would appear to be a driverless vehicle. Steering clear, avoiding, or exercising proper vehicular distancing protocols for each of these situations in my movements in and around our nation's towns and cities is my post-war normal. *Be On the Look Out*, or *BOLO*:

BOLO, white SUV.
BOLO, trash on the road.
BOLO, everything and everybody.
BOLO, the explosion underneath you.
BOLO . . . too late.

But as time progresses and moves me further along rotational time-lines and away from combat-related events that require a defensive reaction as a survival mechanism, these connections to the battlefield slowly evaporate and such slights to my sense of social decorum are less bothersome, at least from the perspective of combat anxiety. I transform. What has been created in me is pushed deeper and deeper into the recesses of my soul, and I remind myself that these are not my enemies, that these vehicles do not wish me harm, that their cars are not laden with explosives ready to plow into me and the trash in the road is not there to hide the presence of freshly overturned dirt under which lies hundreds of pounds of explosives intent on ending my life. These are in fact the behaviors of the freedom-loving people I have sworn to defend. These situations are but temporary assaults on my senses. The light will soon turn green, or the big truck will pass me, and I will be free of these annoying but harmless ambushes and to once again be free in the peaceful existence I have tried to carve out in the freedoms of our homeland.

This same concept can be applied to firework celebrations. Around the six-month mark of a return home I have found I am once again able to attend such celebratory events and know that the explosions I see and hear are of no direct danger. I begin to once again recognize these fireworks as a celebration of some sort that I have chosen to attend utilizing my own civic free will. And it does indeed help if I have chosen to attend the celebration of my own accord. If I can physically see the fireworks in the distance rather than being surprised while alone in my bedroom trying to read or catch up on much needed sleep as my neighbors, tough pyrotechnic warriors they invariably must be, defy local ordinances and play bottle rocket wars in what I am sure must be a purely patriotic celebration of our nation's independence, then I find myself much more at ease. I would further argue that if you are not man enough to handle real explosives in service to our nation than you likely cannot be relied upon to safely operate explosives next to my bedroom window that you purchased at a roadside stand. I am just not sure you have earned the right to fill the void of masculinity in your life by detonating pyrotechnics next to my window while I attempt to read in my bed free of the memories of the many nights I have spent waiting for the moment an actual rocket lands in my lap.

But my neighbors' behavior notwithstanding, the fact remains that even the planned for and fully expected fireworks may still trigger a subconscious response, a reminder of something specific from my combat experience that needs to be further pushed down and hidden deep within my soul. For the most part, I can remind myself that these are celebratory explosions meant to denote the establishment of our nation's independence. Or that this is a celebration of the rotation of the earth around the sun and these explosions and noises are the visual representation of my compatriots' feelings about this natural celestial event. And, in truth, the further away I am from direct combat experiences the more I have to remind myself to cringe at loud noises or to act disturbed by firework displays because this is what combat veterans are supposed to do. And I never want to let someone down in their expectations of combat veterans. But time does indeed have a way of healing the rift in a soul that makes CHRIST necessary. Fireworks and vehicles and piles of trash in the road, however, are the least of my worries.

The real issue boils down to the fact that as part of my creation as a soldier my nation has gone to great length to ensure that I am in possession of instinctual tendencies that force me to intervene and correct rude behavior. It is, I can only presume, the reason I was created. Our nation points out to me another nation that has been rude and then sends me and those that make up the ranks of our nation's military to stop such rude behavior. My CHRIST is not in the business of stopping or changing these instincts, only saving me from those instincts. CHRIST is a counterbalance to my soldierly nature, fighting the baser nature that was instilled in me with my creation. In my nation's military I command respect via rank and experience. In combat I command respect via superior firepower. But in our homeland, respect for your fellow man, like power, is in a constant state of chaotic flux, easily tossed aside in the name of individual liberty. This state of flux, coupled with my inability to exert power the way I have grown accustomed to as a soldier in service to my nation, makes CHRIST a necessary presence in my forays into civilian life, a salvation for a soul riddled with the anxieties that naturally accompany the instincts originating in my creation.

So the real problems arise when I am directly faced with the rude behavior of an individual that I have been trained to suppress in entire countries. Back in our homeland I have no control over rudeness. I am trapped. This is when CHRIST most prominently enters the picture, serving as both comforting guide used to save me from my own creation as well as exacerbating the torture that is the division inside me that must be reconciled. It is in these moments when I cannot escape a situation, when I feel cornered and powerless by my fellow freedom-loving countrymen, that prove the most problematic. I can neither escape the situation nor enjoy the protection provided by the power, the law, the order, and the discipline provided by my military training. I have become a prisoner in my own nation and there is nothing to be done about it.

One of the first incidents in which the presence of CHRIST in my life was evident occurred following an altercation at a town park provided for the sole purpose of dogs to safely play together. I would not generally be in favor of these parks. I regret the fact that I was forced to utilize such a place for the exercise of my own canine. Yet here I was, in an already unnatural situation.

It was at one of these parks that I engaged in a verbal altercation with a young man, a young man I assume loves our nation as much as anyone reading this, who had a problem regarding the level of interaction my dog was allowed to have with his dog. During this verbal altercation I hardly said a word to this young man, imploring him to leave me alone and to go back to his life. I walked away as best I could from this young man no fewer than three times as he continued to badger and follow me until I made it out the exit gate, to my car, and returned home. I refused to argue with the man. I refused to try to explain anything to him. I did not loudly attack him with such words as *pussy* and *bitch* as he used against me. He initiated our unfortunate confrontation with a glare, a flex of his latissimus dorsi, and the command for me to *control your dog*. But my dog was in fact under complete control and this was in fact a park designed for dogs to play together. He had apparently come to the park to allow his two dogs to play only with each other. No other dog should or would be allowed in their vicinity in accordance with his personal and individual foreign policy regarding canine borders. The only defense I will offer in his favor is that, while I was never belligerent *per se*, my initial reaction to his concern for my dog playing with his dog—as he implored, *control your dog*—was for me to tell him to *shut the fuck up*. This is a clear example of my instinctual nature rearing its ugly head and an admonition I have used countless times in day-to-day military operations, in training, and in combat itself. His actions I perceived to be rude and demonstrated a misunderstanding of the purposes of dog parks. So I responded in the way I had been created and subsequently trained by the machine. This young man, however, did not recognize nor appreciate my lifetime of training. So as the situation escalated, I again remembered that civilians do not naturally know, nor can they surmise, my military rank based on my demeanor, nor do they take terse admonishment with the same attitude as young soldiers. It became clear that this was a no-win situation for me. A physical altercation, a street brawl as it were, which is what this situation was moving towards at an alarming pace, is always a crapshoot. I do not care who you are, how often you have been in the ring, or how many action movies you have seen, an unsanctioned fight in a public place is a no-win proposition.

Once this young man continued to escalate the situation, I contained myself and hardly spoke. These are the internal processes at work in my CHRIST. In evaluating the situation, I distinctly remember the young man's lip quivering and exactly two eye twitches that told me he was very scared indeed. And why else would he have acted like this unless he were very scared? Fear is the catalyst for all confrontations. So throughout the event I knew exactly where everyone else in the dog park was, I reached a heightened sense of awareness in my surroundings, moved to a place where everyone in the park was in front of me, maintained full view of my area of operations, and faced this young man directly should his own fear and insecurity cause him to behave erratically.

Of course, he continued to run his mouth. And I waited. I waited in the stillness of time feeling the earth move beneath me. This is combat patience. I knew that fighting this young man over the behavior of dogs was not the right fight. I would lose. I was not likely to lose physically—not that I would admit that to you—though that, of course, is always a possibility as the chance of my gaining overwhelming dominance was slim, and anyone can get lucky and get in a knockout blow in an impromptu street fight. My only course of action if forced into an actual physical fight with this man would be to preemptively strike the moment I saw he was crossing from the mere verbal and into the physical. The moment his demeanor changed and his lip stopped quivering would signal the guttural transition deep within that means fear has completely taken over his body. I would need to strike hard and strike fast, then close off my personal borders with a wall, going into passively offensive mode while awaiting the next progression of our combat. Would the fight be broken up by bystanders? Perhaps. But if not, I would need to re-evaluate, continue to strike if necessary, and maintain the offensive. All of these factors are beyond my control in a so-called street fight and not worth the efforts they claim on a true fighting man. To guarantee a win much more maneuvering would have to be done for me to get into proper position, to prep the battlefield, to set the stage for an engagement in which the odds were overwhelmingly in my favor.

Naturally, the young man continued to berate me until I gathered up my dog and left the confines of the dog park with, at least to this young man and probably to many bystanders, my tail tucked between my legs. But I left because it was the only course of action I could reasonably take. This is my *Civilians in Homeland Reaction and Interaction Syndrome Transfiguration* demonstrating its presence in my life, reining in the instincts that have become part of my created nature, and extricating me from a situation. CHRIST took hold of my heart and enveloped me in the calm demeanor I needed to remove myself from the moment.

This is not to say that my CHRIST is not a tortuous process in my soul. Because while my CHRIST saved me in this example, these events continue to torment me throughout my life. I am convinced this young man has never thought of our altercation once since then. I, however, have thought of it daily, letting it stick in my brain, wondering what I should have done instead, wondering why I let a dog-park tough-guy call me a *pussy* and a *bitch*. I have likely parachuted at the behest of my nation's army from more aircraft than he has actually flown in. I have likely shot more people from countries deemed adversarial by my nation than he has ever met. But the question remains, gnawing at my soul, eating away at my created essence: Am I in fact a *bitch* and a *pussy*? Did I allow my honor to be besmirched in front of a crowd? Was he simply baiting me into assault charges? These are all just replacement questions for the real questions lingering across the many borders within and that haunt me throughout my post-combat life: Should I have flanked the other way during that firefight? Should I have called for mortar fire sooner? Was my letter of condolence to that soldier's parents sufficient?

Now, I wish my CHRIST was the type of syndrome that allowed me to unleash, to go completely berserk, to pummel these colossal boors into the shit- and piss-saturated grounds of municipal dog parks around our nation. But my CHRIST is different. My CHRIST takes my original and immediate response to stimuli based on my creation—the telling of an offender to *shut the fuck up* or to otherwise stop their behavior—calculates the efficacy of further action, then compels me to stand down in the moment. Nothing about CHRIST changes who I am as a person, a man committed to a lifetime of projecting my nation's foreign policy around the globe. My CHRIST intervenes, yes, but in its mysterious way it still allows me to fester and brood for years, leaving me to fret over every decision and action I have ever taken, no matter how innocuous, and turns my created nature into something else entirely. My CHRIST is not in the business of preventing my original mistake but rather of atoning for that action so that it does not escalate to a point of certain regret or pain. And while my CHRIST is always there ensuring my safety, CHRIST does demand work on my part by way of being open to the action, of knowing I am helpless without the syndrome's intervention. This reining in of my instincts, this transfiguration, must come at a price. Salvation always requires sacrifice.

In many of these moments, the interactions in question can present an even more real and challenging element to my wellbeing, making me long for the days when my CHRIST was never a necessity and I lived my life in the dark cloud of constant combat with everything around me.

In yet another instance, while checking out at one of our nation's large department stores, a group of buzzed-but-well-on-their-way-to-full-drunkenness young men got in line behind me. One of the men began singing loudly while standing not more than one foot behind me. He was singing the words to a popular song, a song I have heard many times before and since, a song about love and longing.

Likely, you along with 99 percent of our country's population would have laughed off this breach of social decorum. You might have said *oh, they're having fun, what business is it of mine* and moved on with your life. But my instincts welled up in the moment of rudeness, and I became incensed by the encroachment of this loud, drunken person onto my right to a pleasant, uninterrupted check-out experience within the confines of my own bubble of individual liberty. I kindly asked him to stop singing in my ear at the checkout. This is what I am telling you I told him. You may choose to believe me or not based on what you know of me by now. Regardless, I experienced the instinctual reaction to rudeness that has been implanted in me. Naturally, as you might have guessed, the request from me was not well received by the three young men who then proceeded to ask me to meet them outside.

My CHRIST quickly took over in this moment and I began to plan my escape knowing full well I stood little chance against three drunken louts, and upon further assessment that the numerous bystanders could not be counted on as allies in an altercation. The ringleader of the group asked if I was in the military, a question he surely already knew the answer to based on the cut of my hair and the fact that we were in what has come to be known in our nation as an *army town* in what is a region of our nation in which a large concentration of such towns exist. When I replied that *yeah, I'm in the army*, the young gentleman in question replied:

"Then shouldn't you be overseas getting blown up with your friends, you fucking asshole?"

I can, in fact, do many things post-combat through my CHRIST which gives me strength. This includes the strength to walk away from these unfortunate moments in time when I am not actively enforcing our nation's foreign policy abroad at the behest of my fellow citizens, the strength to deal with those who do not share the same understanding of freedom's limitations as I, all the while lamenting the loss of the power and strength once wielded so powerfully by me and created in me via many years of training and work inside the machine.

So I say yes, yes now and forever, to this drunken, freedom-loving young man, I certainly should be overseas getting blown up with my friends. And it will be a hell of a lot more ordered, disciplined, and peaceful.

9.

IT IS NOW, HERE in this circle with these village elders, that I call upon my CHRIST for the first time not while in our homeland, not while living out the tiny sliver of my life I call *civilian*, but while in actual combat. A boundary has been crossed. Power is skewed. I must reconcile which side of the reaction and interaction I stand. My eyes are open to possibilities I had not known before. But what am I supposed to do? Lines are blurred in an event that sees an injustice, a rudeness if you will, for which I straddle a border. A trite apology is all I can offer them in the moment. I would venture that this is not the worst thing to happen to them in the grand scheme of war, invasion, conquest, and insurgency. And I know my soldiers will deny that they pissed in the villagers' well. They will deny this to the end. They will say that the villagers made up such a tale and that no soldier from our country would ever commit such a heinous act. Deep down I know this to be false. Deep down I know the villagers are telling the truth. And still my soldiers will deny that this happened. The two or three involved have already gotten together and sworn allegiance to each other to never breathe a word of this. I was a foot soldier once, just like them. And we swear oaths to one another for all manner of ills. And we lie for each other. And we lie to each other. And we will carry these lies to the grave with us—lies of conquests, lies of past assignments and jobs, lies of schools attended, lies of loves, lies of sexual prowess, lies of fights—imaginations run amok. And there are unspoken rules about defending one another and lying to, for, and about one another. I can hold company formations for days on end. I can investigate till blue in the face. It will not make a bit of difference. But this must be addressed, so they know I know. I will investigate and I will hold formation after formation and hope and pray my soldiers stick together on this. I do not want to know who did it. Kill all the insurgents? Yes. Accept some level of collateral damage in the conduct of war? Sure. Piss in their wells? Too far.

War is an ugly thing, but not that ugly. Fighting men should be willing to accept some difficult actions as par for the course. It comes with the territory. But all actions are not equal.

"I will find out who has done this and I will see that they are punished," is all I can say to the elders. I cannot explain to them the way military justice works. I have been told these people are barbaric in their meting out of justice, and I know they would settle for nothing less than a rigorous stoning, a lopping off of the offending mad-pisser's pisser. They may even want a beheading. But they will not have it. And they know this. They get an apology. Why are they just now bringing this up? Shouldn't they have walked the short distance to our outpost to lodge this complaint weeks ago? Am I too upset by the actions of my soldiers? The act constitutes gross misconduct. But I can also see the act as a moment of heinously poor judgment on the part of someone having a bad day. The circumstances for pissing in a well are unknown. Do circumstances matter?

The air is sticky on the back of my neck, steaming hot. I was chilly this morning when I took a piss myself into a tube thrust into the hard desert floor. And now I feel every ray of the sun's intense power. Is it possible these villagers have plans for me and my men that they are not divulging? Is it possible that what they have planned is not a normal morning of three rockets, but a night full of rockets, rockets that have been stashed and hoarded on a border for months, even years, just waiting for the right moment to unleash on the isolated outpost the invaders call home, a sitting duck waiting to be burned to the ground, reduced to one gargantuan burn pit like the one that simmers just outside our compound all day, every day, on this, our tiny outpost of civilization, itself divided between my company of men and the indigenous border police, a beacon of freedom and liberty in this unconquered land?

We still have tea throughout the afternoon and I am offered fermented milk as a form of intoxicant, which I politely decline. Something is amiss. I smoke too heavily, drink too much sugary tea, eat too much bread. Just enjoying the company of the villagers during this meeting proves difficult, my own deep concern for what has taken place gnawing at my core, digging a pit in my gut. It is as if someone has just run me through with a harpoon and is still standing there, drinking tea and eating cookies but still looking right into my eyes saying "What are you going to do? You won't do anything. You already know what you are and what you will always be."

We came. We saw. We pissed in their wells? Maybe I am a *pussy*. An overly concerned war-ethicist, if such a thing can exist. Most people who would fret about such things, much less tell you about them, might in fact be on the sensitive side. The kind of person to walk around a combat outpost sneaking glimpses of a sunset. The kind to read books about whaling before they go to sleep at night. The kind to over-romanticize and overthink the whole endeavor.

The feeling of familiarity I know so well in this land escapes me and I am once again the young adolescent scribbling baseball statistics in the margins of a notebook yet still feeling as if my physical being is being transported to my place inside the walls of Chemera, a grown man standing alone in a desert watching a sunset, a dream of chickens and mountain farms, a transfiguration, an out-of-body experience, yes, but a manifestation of my creation as a soldier, the first evidence of a split in reality.

I hear the first shots ring out as if I am on another planet, echoing in my head, reverberating in the village like a call to meditation by a religious leader in the distance. I am violently thrust back within myself, back to the present, taking notice of the ensuing panic from the men posted in security positions around me. Something is happening.

It is clear we are not being fired upon directly here at our tree, that the meeting with the village elders is not in jeopardy, that we are protected. The elders know this and remain seated, fidgeting with their meditation beads or picking at the dirt in front of them. Someone in our element, someone in First Platoon's AO, is engaged, but until we get an initial report, there is no sense in diving for cover and yelling at one another and screaming in the radio, and even then, we should wait for the always more accurate follow-up report. So far? Five to six individual shots, two bursts of our own machine gun fire, no return fire. Certainly does not sound like a decisive engagement. The requisite radio chatter will arrive in due course.

Five seconds pass. Back within my proper soldier's headspace I stare incredulously at my radioman, who hands me my M4 as we watch the security elements on the four corners that make up the vacant lot in the center of the village scramble for cover, heads on a swivel, eyes wide open.

"Well, okay . . . maybe the little darlings changed their mind and they don't feel like playing today," I say to no one in particular as the awkward silence grows longer. I am beginning to get a little worried, not that anyone can tell, unless my attempt to act nonplussed gives me away. But the elders in the still-intact circle show no sign of concern, as if they have been given stage directions.

It is odd to have still heard nothing. I squash the burning desire to get on the radio and ask questions. When someone knows something, they will tell me. The first sergeant comes around the corner at a jog, his radioman and a fire team in tow:

"Sir! What's going on?"

"I don't know, First Sergeant, heard anything?"

"It came from First Platoon's AO but I can't raise them on the net."

The silence breaks. The M240B, machine gun glory, explodes in the distance, a steady stream of five- to six-round bursts for a full twenty seconds followed by the *tap tap tap* sounds of M4 carbines and the distinct sounds of frenzied firefight yelling. The radio crackles to life.

"Battle Six, this is Battle One-six! Troops in contact! Troops in contact!"

The familiar sound of soldiers on the run, bounding and moving, brought to life in the small hand mic just three feet away, my radioman sidekick and partner right behind me, another world brought forward to mingle and begin the whirlpooling of options. I stand and survey the elders. They look at each other, their heads each making a turn around the circle as if this is what they have been waiting for, as if they knew all along what would happen. But they did not know any more than I knew. They are just ready. And nonplussed by events on the ground. Such is the power of presence.

"What do you got, One-six?" I ask in an open-ended manner to allow the lieutenant to provide me the information he deems most relevant rather than feeling obliged to answer questions of no consequence.

"Sir, we need a medevac. My Seven's dropping down to call it in."

I glance over and see the first sergeant on a knee with his radioman to take the medevac request. He will want to hightail it over there, and rightfully so. The lieutenant continues:

"We responded to initial shots fired by moving . . . break . . . seemed like it came from a position over by, break . . . second squad . . . let it develop . . . didn't want . . . when we arrived . . ."

He cuts in and out as another round of automatic fire let loose and then picked up again as if nothing had happened, the events taking place in a stereo in which the speakers are a kilometer apart.

"Two critical and one unaccounted for. I think I'm fighting three to five enemy. Came in from the south on two trucks . . . that's what . . . so far . . ."

Silence. I make eye contact with my radioman. We both know this sounds ugly. We both know we need to start movement.

The lieutenant comes over the mic again, this time crystal clear, "We disabled one truck but they still have another they're fighting us with. Three to five men. First squad has them pinned, I'm about to flank with an element, over."

His breath picks up as I can tell he is moving onto his new objective. He is kicking butt on the radio, reporting as he can, and is handling himself well in what sounds like his biggest contact to date.

"Fight your fight, Lieutenant. Get after 'em."

More machine gun fire, clearly enemy fire, as the unmistakable crack of AKs and PKMs reverberates through the alleyways and dances in our ears. I suspect the enemy is trying to clear a path for their escape.

"I've got targets . . . laid on . . . from here to the . . ."

He is running. Hard. And his transmissions are again garbled.

". . . Alastor . . . they have . . . break . . . Alastor . . . sir."

There is no point in continuing the conversation with the platoon leader as he has a fight on his hands. I have no idea what he means in talking about Alastor. My radioman looks at me with a look I have never seen before; it is the first time I have seen him panicked, wide-eyed and afraid. He is my radioman precisely because he is calm and collected, and of all the soldiers I have known in my career, I felt as though this young man understood me. He does not let tiny things get to him or make mountains out of molehills. He is mature with a keen sense of when the fight matters and when we are just playing a game of potshot tag. He stares at me and I know something is amiss.

"Hold tight, One-six. We're moving your way."

There is no sense in bogging down the LT with requests for more information. We will start movement his way and react as the situation develops.

"Tell Second to collapse their perimeter and protect our backside, junior."

We report the troops-in-contact to Battalion and get ready for the bombardment of questions. I give them the bare minimum in hopes they will shut up long enough to let us all figure out what is happening. Why does Higher never trust their subordinates to fight? What are you going to do, Staff Officer? Tell me which way to flank? My assets are the same as they have always been. Nothing has changed except that you are still amped from your post-lunch workout and aren't getting fed information fast enough so that you can brief the commander immediately.

I ask my radioman to confirm that I had heard the last transmission correctly.

"Did he mention Alastor for some reason?"

I know First Platoon has a Private First Class Alastor in their platoon. I promoted him in a ceremony right before we left our home country and I remember briefly speaking to him at a machine-gun range back home during pre-deployment training. I remember the moment distinctly, sitting here now, wondering how the lieutenant is bearing up, how his fight is developing, wanting to help but knowing I have to let go, let the young lieutenant fight his fight and learn his lessons. So I take a knee and wait. And think my thoughts.

I spoke to Private First Class Alastor that day on the range not because I was impressed with his shooting. I have no idea how he did on the range. But when his platoon broke for lunch, he sat by himself, eating his MRE and reading. He was reading a book of philosophy. This was endearing. And strange. He was alone and would remain alone and was likely disliked in his platoon. Alastor was choosing a very specific path for himself by reading a book instead of engaging in lies about weekend exploits and drunken debauchery. He was in the active process of establishing a dividing line between himself and his peers. I was in the same boat myself as a young enlisted soldier, forced to choose between two worlds. This made me want to reach out to him and say *This is not the way. You cannot win this fight. They are stronger than you.* He looked normal, in a general sense, though his eyes were a little more spread apart than is typical, not freakishly so but enough for me to notice, as if, should he concentrate and manipulate his sleepy eyes accordingly, he might be able to see two different sides of the world at the same time. During my days as a drill sergeant I would have called him *Flounder Face*, understanding that this is not the right description but sticking to it anyway for comedic effect. But he carried himself like a soldier. I spoke to him only briefly and only in pleasantries. He was much more respectful than most of his peers. He actually stood up when I addressed him and had to be told to stand at ease. He had a lively intelligence evident as soon as he spoke but still possessed that habit so common among the overly smart of speaking to someone by just looking slightly away so as to not lose the train of thoughts hurdling through their brains. The rest of the platoon watched with smug anticipation, waiting for me to turn around after our conversation and roll my eyes in a display of silent solidarity that said *You guys got yourself a real weirdo here, don't you?* I wanted to do that, to sacrifice the one for the gratification of the many. But in a moment of self-discipline I kept myself from turning back towards Alastor's platoon members and walked in the opposite direction, leaving Alastor to his book of ancient philosophy and his platoon in the lurch. Had it been another book, something less heady, something that did not mark him as vulnerable, or had he been sitting with a group and reading and chatting and, had I not personally sensed his supreme loneliness, I might have made fun of him for the benefit of his platoon. But he was most definitely lost, bewildered, and alone. I wonder why he was mentioned on the radio now. In case you are unaware, we do not use names over the radio. Information on the wounded is given via a coded battle roster number.

"That's what he said, sir. I just don't know what he meant. Maybe he said something else and we just heard it wrong?"

I pull out my map and overlays and see the nearest medevac site to their last known location is just outside of town. Assuming he is taking fire from the outskirts of town, this is going to be a problem. I regret this placement for a medevac LZ and immediately start scanning the map for better options. This is a rabbit hole of thought I have to get out of quickly, though. Medevac is the first sergeant's issue with which to contend. I and my lieutenant have a fight to conduct, a fight to win. This is our sacred duty, to fight and win. At all costs. I will check on the medevac grid en route and advise the first sergeant on whether or not to move if it looks like it might still be a hot LZ. The first sergeant is still on the radio and I assume he is gathering info through the platoon sergeant. The elders start to get fidgety and I tell my interpreter to tell them it looks like this means the end of our little meeting for the day. They react as soon as they see me speak to him, not waiting for the translation before they all get up and start walking away. Their ability to read body language, voice tone, and inflection unnerves me in the moment.

I call for the first sergeant and his radioman, who are already on their way over to me, my slightly overweight but still very good artillery lieutenant and his sergeant, and an additional four-man fire team for some extra hands and fresh security, to join me in the movement to First Platoon. I run back through the list in my head for no reason, the last thing that needs to be done right now. It angers me that I did it, procrastinating in a moment that called for combat expediency. Yes, of course, these were all the people that needed to go and would not further crowd the situation. These are the men for this mission. Why am I hesitating? I jump on the radio and reiterate to Second Platoon to collapse their perimeter towards the village center. I fail to give a full contingency plan to the platoon leader. But it is time to get out of here and get moving.

The firing stops. Deathly still across the village. No rounds, no bullets, no yelling, no radio. I start moving at a brisk pace, briefing as I go, establishing the order of movement and the standard security plans. I tell them what we know and what my analysis of the situation is as we make our way to the unknown. I feel as if the entire country can hear me:

"Looks like we got two enemy trucks with five to seven personnel causing a ruckus in First Platoon's AO. I'll lead out, stopping short of where I think they might have some trigger-happy guard elements and get a better grid for their locations before we move on to help secure the LZ and help in the fight if need be."

The first sergeant interrupts. "Sir, Battle One-seven said something about Alastor. We need to talk off-line."

"Not now, First Sergeant."

10.

WAR FIGHTING INVOLVES MANY of what we have come to call *the intangibles*. These are events that cannot be planned beforehand nor fully accounted for afterward. Likewise, many of the concepts and ideas I have presented to you as part of the imaginary statistical baseball game I invented in my youth hinged on intangibles as well. The intangibles in this case were invented by me within the game and bestowed upon my players as I so deemed. Further, I convinced myself that the intangibles could in fact be seen through a close study of the numbers themselves so that they are not in fact intangible but are actually quite evident. It simply takes work on the analyzer's part to reconcile the physical nature of the numbers with the mystical and spiritual aspect of the intangibles evident in a close reading so that the numbers create a reality in which one can finally see, become one with, what has before been considered unknowable. The key to understanding the way the game is played by those players who have the intangibles is to yourself adopt an almost mystical demeanor that belies your own inner anxiety and will to power. You must be selfless, humble, and connected to the game in a spiritual sense, in order to see the intangibles in the numbers themselves, just as the player with the intangibles possesses a certain spiritual connection to the game, caring little if at all for the numbers of the game, at least not in an outwardly visible way.

You see, if one of these players were to openly express his desire to win, said player would tip his hand and give his opponent an exploitable weakness. But by maintaining a quiet dignity that respects himself, his opponent, and the game, he is able to convey a sense of coolness to the proceedings that makes everyone believe he really does not care, yet in reality, his sole mission in life was to see his opponent fail and his team succeed. To appear to try would be beneath him, though he is always in the process of setting himself up to be ready to receive the gifts mystically bestowed upon certain players. Remaining outwardly indifferent, stoic even, places a boundary between himself and his teammates that marks him as a true leader by virtue of this indifference, which is in fact his own unseen and unknowable meaningful engagement.

In this part of my fantasy game, the lack of overt zealousness by my best players rankled the front office and drove the sportswriters mad but endeared the player to his peers and less experienced teammates who did not realize that it was these exact actions which made him the unassuming leader that he was. These are the intangibles. They are a gift to those who can effectively fuse two worlds, the physical and spiritual. Intangibles then become tangible through this fusion, the metaphysical now a physical reality. Two essences of a player have now been made whole in this newly-born cohesion. This fusion can be seen in the statistics by those who have combined the two worlds themselves via recognition of the correlation between statistical ups and downs, shifts in the numbers based on time in the season, and the team's win-loss record and streaks. It is only a fallen, lost, and divided world that cannot recognize this unity and will mistake this intangible quality for aloofness or selfishness. The mistake lies in an over-analysis, in delving too deep into intellectual analysis and missing the players', and their own, larger purpose. To see the statistics in their true proper sense, one must ascertain when a player hit the bulk of his home runs and then juxtapose those numbers with times of batting slumps in teammates or, and more importantly, when a player truly possesses the unseen factors that will unconsciously motivate his teammates, actively working to align his own dip in numbers with an increase in the numbers of his teammates so that the team experiences unity in cooperation rather than an undercurrent of competition among teammates. This is when the analyzer will fully come alive and realize not that the team might do better without the player, but that the player is fully in tune with his fellow players such that these teammates will also recognize the need to increase their own game if this star player suffers a slump of some sort. This represents a holistic approach to the game, symbiosis in the universal order of baseball.

Further, an individual's understanding of the intangibles requires them to be in complete control of every aspect of the game now residing within them. These players must know exactly how many steps it takes them to get from the batter's box to first base or the number of steps and the exact time it takes them to leg out a double. The best players can tell by the sound and feel of the bat hitting the ball or the way in which the ball feels when it is released from their fingers whether or not this would be a hit or an out, a single or a double, a sharp breaking ball or a hanging curve. And in a game such as mine, created and based solely on statistical analysis, numbers are created in accordance with their specific abilities and their own personal nuanced approach to the game. The best players know things that the run-of-the-mill fan in the stands does not care to know as a play unfolds. Your average baseball fan is not counting how many times the baserunner's left foot strikes the ground as he tries to stretch a single into a double. My players and I, however, are doing that exact thing. A player should be able to see an invisible line made by the ball coming off the bat and moving through the gap up the middle between short and second, he should then know how many steps it then takes to reach the apex of this imaginary triangle before the shortstop or second baseman gets to the ball to make a play. He should be able to do this while reading the context clues delivered by the first baseman's reaction to the developing play. But his subsequent decision cannot be made by watching the play unfold directly, only the clues around him that have fed the play from the outset, the positioning of players before the ball went into the field of play, the feel of the ball against the bat, his knowledge of the skills of the fielders against which he is matched, the crowd noise and the noise of his own dugout and the signals given by the first base coach all provide context in which he filters his understanding of what is taking place around him. He may choose to use as many of these clues as he feels is necessary and prioritize as required. Against this he must juxtapose his own pace count and where he is in relation to his steps. All this is boiled down to a matter of a few seconds and can be the difference between a game-changing single and just another out, between the start of a series of events that lead to victory or another chink in the armor that will account for his team's ultimate demise. All this takes place while the average fan sits in the stands unaware of all these events taking place in a matter of seconds. All this takes place as part of the player's creation over many years of practicing and playing the game again and again and again, of finding himself in the same places over and over, the same situations again and again, until he has no conscious say in the matter, his actions are no longer his but rather an offshoot of his part in the bigger machine that is his team. He is good because he executes blindly, and mystically, not knowing how he has come to count his steps but knowing that they must be counted, not knowing how he has come to know how a well-hit ball sounds and whether or not the sound indicates if the ball will veer or hook on its trajectory down a foul line. These are things he just knows, elements of his game one might consider preordained at this point but in fact very much rely on the will of the player to believe in the game, to accept the brilliant nuance inherent in the game's design, and then be open and willing to work to hone these skills to the level evident in the numbers he now puts up. These factors *are* his continuing creation as a ball player. And they are part and parcel of the numbers once exhibited in the divisive margins of an adolescent notebook.

And so the first sergeant stares at me, perplexed by my answer.

"Not now, First Sergeant."

Not now. In the back of my mind I have briefly considered the possibilities that they cannot find Alastor. But he is likely just hiding behind a mud wall, reading his ancient book of philosophy, a conscientious objector exposed in the heat of battle. This is what I want. More than anything else I hope we have a newly-minted coward on our hands who will turn up as soon as the coast is clear, a traitor who hides during dicey firefights. Even better would be if he turns out to be the well-pisser, too. It is not unusual for the most barbaric-acting, the most warrior-posturing, to be consumed with crippling fear when the real bullets start to fly. If he has shirked his duty during a firefight and also been the one to piss in a well? Well, that is the entire day wrapped up in a nice, neat package. This is the best possible scenario for me and my men.

The artillery lieutenant's chin strap is already drenched in sweat. He looks exhausted, wild-eyed, as if he has been in a continuous firefight for two straight days. Despite his lack of fitness, he is still quite good at his job. And, honestly, his slightly pudgy physical demeanor is a trivial matter. He just happens to be one of those guys with a soft face that makes him look a little doughy.

"Sir, we have one-five-five targets laid on just outside of town for ten more minutes. Just need PID and we can shoot. Apaches will be on station in fifteen, where do want them pushed?"

"Away from Jacuz. As close to the border as they can get. They're looking for a white Hi-Lux."

I do not need a description of the truck from the platoon leader in the fight. All trucks in this country are white Hi-Luxes just as Apache attack helicopters are always fifteen minutes away. Our army has figured out the perfect location for attack helicopters throughout the country so that they are always exactly fifteen minutes away from of any skirmish. This is an example of good outpost placement. This knowledge makes me immensely proud of my army and for all the moments in which I question decisions, I take great satisfaction in the possibility that maybe there is a grand scheme to which I am not privy. Perhaps a lowly company commander does not have all the answers, and my superior officers and the politicians know exactly what they are doing, and I should maintain a more positive outlook on the situation. Systems are in place that have operated smoothly, efficiently, for at least two centuries in my own nation and for many centuries before across the span of global warfare history. Perhaps the plan is transparent to me. Or opaque.

I have never questioned my loyalty before but realize, as you may have already recognized, that by questioning everything my superiors do, by applying my pragmatic realism to every aspect of my career, I may be displaying an immense disloyalty to the organization. I am not now wholly committed to this idea but will cede that this is a possibility and is a possibility in which you, dear reader, may have already reached a verdict. What remains unclear to me, though, is whether or not this cynicism is borne out of a career of disappointments, of exposure to mediocrity, or of a subconscious and unbridled need to fight ingrained in my creation and not being given the full opportunity to fight as desired. In the absence of being provided a good fight, I find fights, seek turmoil wherever it might lie, make up issues and incompetency where there is none. So where, then, does the incompetency lie? Perhaps you already know the answer. And I am blind to this truth. Is being unable to function within the system a sign that the system is flawed? The thought smacks me broadside, a mental sucker-punch for which I am ill-prepared. *Not now. For the love of all things holy, not now.* But it weighs on me as we make our way through the shadowy alleyways dodging mangy and vicious dogs—the lead team puts down two dogs en route before I tell them to stop—and curious children following us through the tight turns, meeting us ahead of decisive corners, intuitively knowing exactly where we will turn up next.

Our element moves swiftly through the alleys and streets despite the obstacles. This is a good team; each of us moves with what can only be described as a feeling of divine purpose. We are a unified, singular organism expanding our nation's foreign policy, the bounding and overwatching, the free flow of soldiers representing poetry in motion: fluid, no talking, a sense of the mystically intangible evident in our every move. We are a living entity of interlocking fires expanding our nation's foreign policy influence as we bob and weave through the village. Doing our job. Putting the ball in play. Transcending.

The sun moves with us, just beginning its long, slow, slogging, descent behind the distant horizon, marking just the beginning of the day's closure. Firefights have a special ability to speed the sun along. The earth spins faster in combat. And still, no sound.

We stop to get our bearings and I call First Platoon to get a grid for any security elements we might run into so we do not just plow into a machine gun team and get shot up as we round a corner. Machine gun teams love to crouch in small ditches and in places that offer them no line of sight. I know we will come out of an alley, round a corner, and get lit up by an itchy-fingered gunner lying in a piss-filled ditch with twenty meters of sector in which to engage targets. I hear helicopters in the distance—not the Apaches, the medevac birds—and that's when I hear the voices of soldiers in the distance and know we have overshot our mark. A navigation error based on my propensity for left-handed over-compensation. Those of you with experience will know exactly what this means.

"Hey One-six, you got a good read on the locations of all your men, all your security elements?"

"Negative, sir."

Good answer. He could have given me bullshit grids to his security elements and I would have proceeded with confidence only to run into one of his still antsy machine gunners for whom time was still clipping along at combat speed. He has forced me to proceed with caution.

We are well past due giving Battalion an update and my radioman plays the delay game several times with the company executive officer back at Chemera while we are moving. At one point I hear him say "No more casualties, still in contact," which are the two best things you can say to Battalion to buy some time. We backtrack about a hundred meters and peel off into an abandoned and crumbling house as the choppers close in. I get a refined grid for the LZ, unnecessary at this point, and an update from all the elements. Second Platoon is shifting to the town center. First Platoon is securing the LZ for Medevac. Third platoon back at Chemera is ready to launch if necessary, though we cannot abandon Chemera to be defended by what is left of Headquarters Platoon. The howitzers are off. Apaches are approaching from the east with an ETA of five minutes. I will spend the next two minutes trying to pinpoint the LZ like a rat looking for cheese.

11.

THE MEDEVAC BIRDS BEAR down, and I realize we are much closer to First Platoon than I thought. I am back in my head once again. I take out a small piece of bright orange VS-17 panel stuffed inside my helmet, tighten up my entourage, and start movement, waving the orange panel around each corner so as to not get shot by a nervous gunner. We do not make two corners, fifty yards, when the first wisps of yellow smoke waft across the alley to our left. We turn and run straight into a machine gun team splayed out in a ditch and securing an area for which they have, at best, twenty-five meters of range. They look defeated.

"Where's the LT?"

"Don't know, sir."

We move to the LZ and arrive to disorder, soldiers dashing about in the open field, several huddled around what looked to be two soldiers laid out on the ground, yellow and green smoke billowing, an obvious miscommunication as multiple soldiers must have thrown signal smoke to vector in the birds. Of course, all combat scenes are chaotic from the outside looking in. Only when inside of the fight can you truly understand how the pieces interconnect, the ebb and flow of the work taking place. And there are some endeavors in which a certain degree of disorderliness is the preferred method. Such is the case here, the running about, the yelling, this flow of adrenaline keeps the fight alive in the spirit well after the game has been played out until eventually the whole enterprise collapses in a heap of exhaustion. I need to tie myself into this beautiful controlled chaos without adding to the confusion. I spot the platoon leader and his small group huddled in the far corner of the field and I leave my fire team posted in place as I head over to link up. The first sergeant heads to the casualties to clear out some of the rubberneckers not essential to the evacuation.

Choppers start kicking up dust just as I reach the LT. I can see the casualties are on their feet waiting to get loaded and I recognize them both. Good dudes. Neither of them Alastor. This is not the time to split hairs, but my first question for the platoon leader is why these casualties are reported as critical.

"Sorry, sir. I panicked. Got bad info."

"That's alright. They'll figure it out. You okay?"

"Yes, sir. I'm fine," he says, though I'm not sure I believe him.

The supporting Apache attack helicopters arrive and begin buzzing the town in the exact way they should not. I stand up and glare across the open space at my artillery lieutenant, who is already fixing the situation. If you do not tell an Apache pilot exactly where to fly he will always fly as close to the ground, and to you, as possible, just to piss the ground commander off. The buzzing beasts peel off and head for the border as the medevac birds take off in the opposite direction headed for Palermo. The field grows silent, the men center down into stillness, monuments to a moment, the chaos that was now complete.

I extend my hand to the lieutenant for a handshake and he dutifully stands up and gives me a sad, trembling hand. He is exhausted. His hand floats back down to his side and I offer him a cigarette as we look for a place where we can sit, take our helmets off, and figure out what in the hell is going on.

"I don't know what to do. What do we do?" He asks as he lights his cigarette.

"What do we do about what? You just had a fight. A nasty one. But you've been in fights before. Get your reports together so I can talk to Battalion and we can get this thing worked out. They're starting to breathe down my neck for info."

"Sir, you haven't told them about Alastor? I don't know what to do."

All the color is gone from his face. His hands shake as he brings the cigarette up to his sweaty lips.

"What about Alastor? Was he one of the wounded? Didn't look like it."

"Sir, he's gone. I reported it. I told you in my first radio call. He's been captured."

"What do you mean captured? Captured captured?"

"Yes, sir. POW captured. He's . . . with them."

"What the hell, Lieutenant? What the actual hell? Are you sure he's not just hiding somewhere behind a wall, scared out of his fucking mind?"

"I watched him get in the truck, sir. It was his team that disabled the first truck; then the second truck rolled in and . . ."

I have to interrupt him. I now realize I am quite possibly the only one who did not accept this truth and I react accordingly.

"Jesus H.! You should have been very clear to me on the radio that you had a soldier missing in action. Are you kidding me?"

I threw my helmet into the open field where the smoke grenades left long burnt streaks on the ground and soldiers stood silent, motionless.

"What do we do?"

"The first thing I do is get on the horn with Battalion and report whatever the hell this just became!"

I turn and yell at the dazed and confused statues spread across the LZ

"I want everyone else pulling security. Now, goddammit! Stop being sad clowns and pull security! We have work to do, men!"

I call for the first sergeant, who is already on his way towards me. I was so concerned with letting my llieutenant fight his fight, of being a good leader by letting my subordinates lead, that I refused to get a clear picture of what was going on. These are things that I know to do. And I failed. I failed the lieutenant, the company, and I failed the mission.

We move to a nearby rooftop so my radio operator can throw up his long whip and hopefully get better communication with Battalion through a re-trans station rather than via relay through the company XO at Chemera. Comms are still hit-or-miss and this will only add to the anger and misunderstanding that will ensue as I attempt to relate what has happed here in Jacuz. We have not had good comms since we left the village square, and as I make the call, repeating myself through static, I realize I will not be watching the sunset through the haze of a burn pit this evening. I will not do any reading from my book about whalers pursuing a mighty beast tonight. There will be no tales of revenge and the sea. I likely will not sleep for the foreseeable future.

The S3 answers the radio back at Battalion, a lazy yes-man of a major who feels no love for me. After some back-and-forth I convince him to put the battalion commander on directly. A long pause while I wait for my boss to finally answer.

"Go for Six."

"Roger, sir, our two wounded should be arriving at Palermo in a few minutes, break . . . Not critical, both ambulatory, break . . . More to follow on the nature of their injuries once I get a thorough backbrief from the platoon sergeant, break . . . We have one man currently missing. I'm directing platoons to . . ."

He interrupted me:

"Break. Break. Break. Say again last."

I said again . . . and waited.

"You lock down that entire village immediately, captain. No one moves, no one leaves. No one. Move those Apaches to start scanning every egress route from Jacuz into the mountains and await further guidance. Do you understand?"

Of course I understand. I understand that we are missing a soldier and nobody will know how to deal with this. I also understand that any reaction is knee-jerk and will be made by those with no knowledge of the terrain or of what had just happened, a check-the-box, by-the-numbers reaction because *this is what you do, this is how you signal that you are doing . . . something.* I understand that this is what we have to do to satisfy Higher, but whether or not anyone believes this to be an effective measure remains unclear. Sometimes actions and orders in the army feel as though upper leadership is watching a different movie than the rest of us. I am sure Alastor is no longer on this side of the border. I do not know where he is, of course, but I do know he is no longer on our side of an international border about which no one but our nation is concerned. He has been removed from a country at war with an insurgency to a country pretending to not be at war. But they will not harm him, not significantly, anyway. A soldier from our nation is much too valuable a prize for the enemy. They will use Alastor to their advantage. But I reply the only way I can.

"Yes, sir."

I drop the hand mic by my side, slump, look at my radioman, then off into the distant stars.

"Well, fuck me."

My radioman smirks and confirms,

"Yes sir, fuck us."

I direct the men to lock down the village. I have no recollection of taking this action, of who I speak to, or how the lockdown is coordinated. It is just suddenly dark and no one is around me. But this cannot be true. My men must be nearby. I would not abandon myself like this nor isolate myself from my men. I strain my eyes and shake my head to snap out of my environment and there they are, a smattering of men on a rooftop—twelve soldiers in our nation's army—some in security positions, some eating portions of MREs, one inexplicably pissing off the roof into the alley below.

In my first firefight, many years prior, my platoon was ambushed during a short halt for a map check. I dropped the map into a ditch, returned fire, moved and communicated, the map forever lost to the battlefield. When you are ambushed, maps no longer matter, places change, the space you inhabit cannot be represented on any map, real places never are. Your newfound reality can no longer be contained on a graphical representation of the earth's surface as seen from above but rather in the new experience exploding in your brain. This was the first of many ambushes, many fire-fights, many rockets, morning and night. They are all the same, and you reach a point in the fight when a map is no longer useful. And then a new fight rears its ugly head. And all you want is a map of some sort. Earlier to-day the village elders told me a soldier pissed in their well and I am brought back to reality, brought back to my own body on this rooftop, watching a soldier piss from the roof onto the street below.

"Hey dumbass, unless you want me to throw you off of this roof, you better put your shit away right now and quit pissing off this roof."

He ignores me and I am not in the mood.

"I swear to God, son . . ." and I start my move toward him, ready to throw him off the roof and down into the dark piss-stained alley below as payment for every rocket I ever took cover from, every ambush I have ever experienced, for every soldier I once knew who was no longer a part of our world but now existed elsewhere in the eternity of soldier's time. I was tossing him off the roof for relieving himself. I was tossing him off the roof for my nation and for Alastor. I was even tossing him off the roof for you, dear reader. The first sergeant is in front of me within two steps, grabbing me by the shoulders and yelling. I do not hear what he says. I did not know he was anywhere near me. All I know is that right now, a soldier under my charge is missing, and a part of my body is gone.

I cannot parse apart what is happening to us, like reading one of my books for which I have no frame of reference but through which I must press on. The events of the last twenty-four hours are trash in a burn pit, stirred shit in a steel can.

12.

0120. THE RADIO CHATTERS with activity as platoon leaders send in report after report. I make continual updates with Battalion.

"All locked down."

"No change."

"Light flash in the mountains, grid to follow, push drone to scan area."

The battalion commander is in meetings with the brigade commander and his staff, and they will be here in Jacuz before daybreak. Keep the town locked down, nothing comes in and nothing goes out. Half our military is mobilizing towards us to help lock down the AO, the other half is rerouting their own patrols and missions in a nationwide search for a soldier who is no longer in this country but has crossed a border no one talks about.

We are invaders and conquerors of a foreign land, each of us a representation of our nation's foreign policy projected to the maximum effective range of our personal weapon systems. Yet the only thing that keeps each and every one of our combat outposts from being overrun is the indifference of the people, people who have been invaded many times over the course of hundreds of years and have still never been conquered. I only just now realize that indifference is the wrong word. They care deeply. But they know better than we that their connection runs deeper, rings truer to this land than ours. We never really invaded in the way others have. My nation has never conquered anything. We blanket with a thin sheet, saturate with ideas and concepts, never conquer. This is a subtle difference but a difference nonetheless. Time has never been on our nation's side, a beacon on a hill whose soft light reached the world before its influence could be properly established, a grand idea and thought with no backing substance, a flash in the pan, tinkling brass, a global money laundering operation.

Being locked down, surrounded by foreign soldiers, will not sit well with the people of Jacuz. They do not care because they know too much.

They know how our timeline works, know we will eventually leave, tired and bored, that our thirst for power has a shelf date. They know us to be fickle and short-sighted and by simply waiting us out—letting small bands of reactionaries and guerrillas, those we have come to call *insurgents*, attack in small coordinated ambushes, and letting them plant roadside bombs, and allowing them to launch rocket attacks on our bases from the safety of international borders—we will eventually leave and look for power elsewhere.

My two platoons here on the ground easily shut down Jacuz and keep these people from leaving. They do not even try. They just move on with their lives. If you bring me one more platoon, we can search every home in this village with ease. We can tighten the screws here unlike anything done in the rest of the country. Finally. It's a tragedy that it has taken a missing soldier to spur action, but we can do in this country what we have been trained to do: destroy this nation because this nation has wronged us in one way or another. We let the insurgency happen. Only we can shut it down.

But, foolish nation of ours, Private First Class Alastor is not in Jacuz. Yet these are my orders and I intend to carry them out. *Disrupt*. Now *Isolate*.

"We have a job to do, men."

We are to maintain this posture until the battalion commander and his staff arrive. Drones have been pushed to the border and units from across the country are re-missioning to head our direction. From what I can gather from information the executive officer was getting back at Chemera, the entirety of our nation's army is in crisis mode, locked down and conducting change of mission operations to find Alastor.

Did the XO see to it that the trash at Chemera was burned last night? Did he sleep at all? Did the rest of Headquarters and Third Platoon pull stand-to? What is Alastor doing right now?

The village elders are now congregating below the roof of this house demanding answers. This took longer than I thought it would. They look alien in the moonlight, visitors from a distant galaxy. They say they cannot sleep in their homes with soldiers all around them.

"Well, welcome to my world," and I have to quickly tell my interpreter not to translate this. They say we displaced the family of the home whose roof we are occupying right now.

"You've gotta be kidding me. So what?" Again, do not translate that. These elders know what is going on and are playing a victim game with me. They can wait. If they suffer some mild discomfort in the interim, so be it. I am in no mood for their antics. I have lost power and now intend to get it back. I will not entertain their petty squabbles and supposed affronts to their dignity.

Alastor's platoon leader climbs the steps to the roof and walks my direction. He is alone and says he needs to talk to me, which I am always happy to do. A good kid. A bright, young officer, motivated, earnest, but keeps his aspirations well-hidden. I feel bad for him. I feel bad that I lost my cool and yelled at him earlier. This is his first combat tour and up until now, he has never had a man evac'd for a serious injury, much less lost one. Exhaustion reads across his face.

"Sir. I need to tell you, need you to know and make sure you understand that Alastor wasn't captured."

"Dude. What the fuck are you talking about?"

"He ran to them with his arms up. He surrendered. I saw him myself."

"Stop, Lieutenant. You're tired. Go get some sleep over there by my stuff. I'll wake you in an hour or so."

"Sir, I'm not kidding. I tried telling you earlier. His team disabled the first truck. They were like fifty meters from it. And when the enemy got out to try and join the second truck and started running away, Alastor ran out in the middle of the firing and joined them. Just ran right up to them. It was like they were here to pick him up. But that can't be. I didn't say anything because everything was so crazy and I couldn't believe what it was I saw, and to be honest I'm still not sure. But I know I'm not crazy. I talked to the guys he was with and they confirmed it and the guys around me said the same thing."

"Not a word, Lieutenant. Not a single word until we figure this out. The boss is coming here at first light and I assume another company or two to start clearing operations. I also assume other elements will move in close to the border and try and get it locked down. Too little, too late, but whatever. We know Alastor is across the border. But for right now, I don't want a word of this breathed to anyone else. Do you understand me?"

"Sir."

"Do you understand me?"

"Yes, sir. But we have to tell them, don't we?"

"Why? Will we just say *Ah, forget it then* and leave Alastor with them? Do you think the way he ended up in enemy hands makes any difference whatsoever? It does not. This entire occupation just came to a halt until we find our kid. Regardless of how he was lost. Go brief your men that they keep their mouths shut until we figure out what actually happened . . . internally. Then we can let the staff whackers know. There's going to be the biggest investigation either of us have ever seen. I promise you that. This is huge. Fucking huge. Heads will roll. But let's figure this out in-house first. When you're done with that go shut your eyes for at least an hour."

These are the wrong words and I know it. This is not the path to follow and the only recourse is to be completely honest on all fronts. But right now I can think of no reason to believe that a soldier has voluntarily given himself over to the enemy. And since I cannot wrap my head around the possibility, I assume it can never happen.

"And I'm sorry I yelled at you earlier. You did everything right. Good job today."

"Yes, sir, thank you."

"I mean, it would have been nice if you had killed the enemy, maybe disabled *both* trucks. You know? Something? Anything? Come on, man."

"Sir, they came flying in, guns a-blazing. I was taking a squad and flanking around and that's when . . ."

"Stop. I'm fucking with you. This is real bad. Now go to sleep."

So now I am to believe Alastor left of his own volition? To what purpose? A new narrative to digest. Such as it is. This will change nothing, of course, may make matters worse as the soldiers will lack the ability to muster any goodwill for a deserter from our army, an army we all love beyond measure, an army that is part of a nation we love. There are rules against such actions. And we are nothing without rules. Further, shutting down every mission and reallocating our nation's assets into finding this lone soldier will only breed resentment. A balance will have to be sought between making a real effort and when to call that effort off, when to return to a sense of normalcy in our mission. We are going to screw this up and I suddenly recognize pangs of hunger in my gut. I pull my meal from my assault pack and slowly, methodically, graze on the peanut butter and crackers while drifting away from my place here on this rooftop, mentally separating as the commander of these men, drifting across the village, hovering in place, until I float slowly into the dark sky in remembrance of a different time and place in my youth, the taste of dry cracker and peanut butter satisfying, energizing, like the first bite of a favorite meal back home.

13.

CROUCHED ON THIS DUSTY rooftop, the cool dark of the night sky envelops me and I am suddenly back at my favorite restaurant as a child, a place that I have long since forgotten the name of but which called itself a *restaurant and boarding house* and which likely no longer exists and which likely never existed as a boarding house at all, at least not a boarding house as we have come to know now but which at the time I thought was in fact a boarding house so that in my childhood I thought a boarding house was a type of restaurant in which you sat at long tables and the meals were served family style and the waitresses wheeled out plates of fried chicken, dumplings, mashed potatoes, collard greens, corn bread, and a strange gelatinous desert with a pie crust over the top I have not seen since.

The interior walls of this *restaurant and boarding house* were covered in vintage posters from entertainment events performed in our home country during a previous era: traveling circuses, wild frontier shows, ribald theatrical performances. We ate here out of what must have been my parent's sense of nostalgia for a bygone past, when our nation was much different and apparently the citizens of our nation spent much of their time attending circuses, wild frontier shows, and ribald theatrical performances. My parents were not old enough to have experienced anything depicted in the posters, yet their false sense of nostalgia became my actual lived experience. What they considered nostalgia was in fact the building blocks to my youth as I was much too young to understand their nostalgia as anything other than my present.

There was no individual ordering at this *restaurant and boarding house*, as there was no menu that I recall. The same food was served every week. You either ate what was put in front of you or you went without. We had to drive a great distance to this restaurant, a drive in which the specifics escape me, as does the catalyst for our attendance. We were just there. It just happened. I only know it took a long time to get there because I overheard such information many years later when my parents spoke of the place fondly. Driving down the long, gravel driveway and seeing the first images of the old weather-worn farmhouse with the wraparound porch are my only real memories of the journey. This was a *restaurant and boarding house* suspended in space in an ocean of loblolly pines and moss-draped oaks.

I miss this restaurant right now as I eat MRE peanut butter and crackers on this roof in a foreign land. But me missing this restaurant is really just a longing for my own parent's misguided nostalgia, a nostalgia which might have been triggered by a place where they ate in their own youth, which might have later come to them on a dark rooftop in a foreign land while they ate a snack. Though I do not know that my parents would have ever had reason to eat a snack on a rooftop in the dark. One never knows these things, though, do they? The history of nostalgia, that is. And whether or not it has ever been real.

I execute a series of long, slow blinks, waking with a start and half-eaten, crumbled cracker in my lap. Everyone on the rooftop, save two machine gunners in opposite corners, are sprawled out in various states of repose. My radioman is curled in the fetal position under his poncho, hand mic next to his ear. I tilt my head back against the wall and fall asleep. The ship's deck still and silent in the dark ocean.

0525. My radioman, yelling from under his poncho, wakes me with the message that the battalion commander is on the way.

"Siiiiiir. Birds inbound with the big boss man."

I need to get myself and a squad out to the LZ to meet him and the rest of the staff. ETA fifteen minutes. I was not looking forward to this. My radioman gets up slowly, but, once fully standing, spins into a flurry of activity, packing his gear away, ready to go, posted right behind me in seventeen seconds flat as I rush to get my poncho put away and don my gear.

"That's a tie."

"Bullshit, sir, I beat you."

"Whatever, little camper."

I ask my radioman what Alastor is like.

"He's cool. A little weird. Smart as fuck though. And quiet. They call him *Beluga* in the platoon because one time during combatives he got pissed and head-butted a team leader in Second Platoon and the team leader said it was like he had an extra fucking lump on his forehead just for butting people. Which, I don't know if that makes sense, but then the platoon just started calling him that, I think more because he's kind of an egghead anyway and reads a lot. But I like him. I actually thought he'd make a good replacement for me when the time came for me to go back to the line."

It is good to put a face, a name, a personality to a soldier. I wish I knew Alastor better, but frankly, despite my best efforts, the bulk of an officer's time during training in our home country is spent on mounds of paperwork or dealing with problem soldiers—those who cannot keep their hands off their wives, or other people's wives in a different manner of speaking, and the smattering of druggies and drunk drivers that constitute 10 percent of the ranks but take up 90 percent of our time. The nickname bestowed upon him, *Beluga*, reminds me of a fellow I went to officer school with who had a sort of forward-sloping forehead that protruded in the front. We called him *Logarithm* as an inside joke, as if an overdeveloped part of his brain had emerged, causing his forehead to slope forward a bit and rendering him particularly adept at complex mathematical function. In hindsight, *Beluga* would have been a good nickname, too. Once, at an officer social function, *Logarithm* ordered a hot water and a teabag, which prompted me to make the case that his name should be changed to *Teabag*, though it never stuck.

It is comforting to know my radioman likes Alastor. The task at hand becomes much easier. We would exert the same effort for anyone, but at least psychologically I am not searching for an asshole in a haystack. I am simply looking for a deserter.

I yell down to the first squad leader I see and get him and his squad spun up to pop out into the big open area. It will be a close call getting an area properly secured in time. I hustle down the roof and we all make it down to the LZ just as the birds make radio contact. Nothing is secure, but we are getting there. The squad leader has just made it out and throws some IR chems down for markings, though we know the pilots do not pay any attention to such things, they just want to know that the area is secure. Sure, secure as it's ever been.

Sixteen men stumble out of two utility helicopters. For most, this is the first time they have ever left the confines of their staff offices, and it shows. Maps, boards, laptops, fresh clean uniforms, brand new chinstraps, and freshly bloused, clean aftermarket boots—staffers always buy the most expensive boots for walking back and forth to the mess hall and the gym—weapons dangling from their necks via long, ill-adjusted slings.

The battalion commander surprises me. I did not immediately recognize him among the entourage milling about the LZ, heads on a swivel, looking for a place to take a knee because that's what they think you are supposed to do. He was in my face, yelling louder than necessary after his short flight, asking me where he is supposed to set up. "Follow me, sir," and I sense that he's displeased, as if he expected me to have an operations center set up for him on the LZ. The gaggle falls in behind him like ducks in a row, and we move to the rooftop where I find my soldiers in varying stages of undress and guard posture.

The first sergeant is up and running around, making the situation far worse than it needs to be. It is painfully obvious that this is what our soldiers do after a long night of locking down a village. Any effort to run around and get boots bloused and gear put away rings phony, an obvious afterthought meant to impress a lieutenant colonel.

The commander offers his hand, and I remember this exchange of power dynamics when I exercised it upon my own platoon leader. I appreciate the down-to-earth gesture but am still braced for the dressing down I am about to receive.

"Alright, Company Commander. Talk to me. What happened?"

I give him the rundown of the past twenty-four hours, conveniently glossing over the part where Alastor might have voluntarily gone missing.

He starts in:

"Okay, I have your buddies over in Basla coming to help lock down the village. The brigade commander has moved additional assets this way to lock down all egress routes out of your AO. We have just about every drone asset in the arsenal in your AO right now, I'm sure the Big Six is in his TOC right now watching us have this discussion on Pred feed. For now, continue to hold steady, nothing comes in or out of this village. I don't know if your men are feeling sorry for themselves or what, but you need to get them off their asses and get them to work, Captain. You'll be here for the indefinite future. Hell, I'll be here too. This just became ground zero for the entire operation. Understood?"

He did not mention the border less than five kilometers away. He does not seem to really take into account the relatively small size of Jacuz and the fact that we have had it easily locked down all night. He does not seem to understand that my men and I came over here for a day patrol and are ill-provisioned for long-term operations. He does not seem to understand that Chemera is just a short hour's walk away and that it would do my men a hell of a lot of good to go back and refit, to get our bearings, once the company from Basla gets in here to take over.

"Sir, the firefight happened right here on the outskirts. The men saw the truck Alastor was in, and it took off for the foothills and the border. I'm betting he's well across the border by this point."

"I already got your rundown. I don't need your analysis. Have you ever had a soldier missing before? I didn't think so. I don't give a rip if you think Alastor's at the bottom of the sea right now. I told you what to do. I told you what was happening. Now execute."

"Yes, sir."

I am tired and have to remind myself that he's always been fair to me. That he is, for all intents and purposes, an excellent battalion commander. I can see the stress in his eyes, though, stress mostly caused by the prospect of losing his military future, his meticulously outlined career path, at the hands of a jackass, prior-enlisted-man-turned-officer company commander that just lost a soldier. But he means well.

Glancing around the rooftop I spot the first sergeant in conversation with the command sergeant major. I skulk away from the commander and slink towards the first sergeant, the S3 smirking at me as I move across the rooftop. *Fuck you*, I want to say and flip him off just for the hell of it. What are they going to do me? Make me stay in Jacuz looking for a deserter who is not here? Of course, I don't do it. In this instance I am much too institutionalized, a company man who hates the company he is in.

This too shall pass.

14.

ON ONE OF MY previous trips to this country I led a platoon of paratroopers as part of a larger operation involving the clearing of a small city, building by building, house by house. We were to start at one end of the city and work our way through our assigned sector for several nights, our sister platoons on either side of us, in their respective sectors, until the job was done. My platoon was inserted with the rest of the company via helicopter in a large poppy field on the outskirts of the city, and from here we were to branch off with pre-designated resupply and linkup points scattered throughout the operation. The initial clearing was to take seventy-two hours followed by several days of establishing our presence and growing our footprint in the AO. It was a dicey mission and the men were excited.

My platoon had been getting after it nonstop since we got off the birds earlier in the night—potshots here and there, some small ambushes, a few cuts and scrapes, some minor shrapnel wounds—but we pressed on. The boys were tired but still amped, and we continued to breeze through the objective, kicking in doors, searching homes, wreaking havoc. At around *0300*, just as we finished clearing another section of homes and were still in our own little clusterfuck trying to get the order of movement sorted so we could get to the next checkpoint, the lead team rounded a corner and started a frenzied yelling, a cacophony of screams:

"Halt! Freeze! Get down, motherfucker! Stop! Hands up!"

Soldiers think that by yelling as loud as possible at a local they will suddenly understand our language. This idea is further exacerbated after a long night of room clearing. So the patrol was halted in a pretty dicey alleyway, we were already in disarray, and I wasn't real comfortable with the situation as I made my way to the front to see what was happening.

When I got to their position I found they already had some poor guy down on the ground with four dudes on top of him. He was writhing around, screaming, making god-awful noises like he was possessed. The squad leader told me that this guy just came wandering out of the alley with his hands up holding something and mumbling gibberish. By all rights, the kids could have pulled the trigger, dropped him right there. He could have had anything in his hands, a detonator, grenade, anything. But the closest soldier decided the guy was already too close anyway and just ran and pounced on him. Turns out, he had a half-eaten pear in one hand, prayer beads and a notepad in the other. This notepad was full of drawings of trucks and planes and helicopters and explosions that loooked like a five-year-old drew them. So they got the guy all cuffed, both hands and feet, and got him to sit up so I could talk to him.

But when I started talking to him through the interpreter, this dude looked as happy as I have ever seen another human being. His eyes were lit up, he was smiling like crazy, and the interpreter could barely make out what he was saying. Finally, the interpreter turned to me and said,

"I think this guy is not so smart."

I suddenly realized we had just captured the goddamn village idiot. But the men had been awake at this point for nearly twenty-four hours, one scare after another, and they contended that this guy's notepad was full of terrorist plans. His beard was caked with dirt, mostly fresh from our guys throwing him around on the ground. He didn't smell too good and he was smiling so much he was starting to drool. Young too. Somewhere in his twenties perhaps. But I couldn't let this go now, as the report of a captured enemy combatant had already been pushed higher. They would want better answers than *Oh, never mind, we think he was not so smart.* And I couldn't tell my guys *Nice work, you captured the village lunatic* as some of them were still convinced he's an insurgent, that he was putting on an act. So at *0330* I made the decision to just roll with it. We'd push him higher on the first re-supply bird we could get in here, and they could figure it out for themselves. I told the men they're doing great things and to go ahead and undo his feet and that I'd secure him in the middle of the patrol with me. "Let's keep moving," I said, "We'll process him when we get to our next checkpoint."

So I took him to the center of the patrol and he was still grinning ear to ear, taking it all in. The guys around me in the patrol were getting angry with me, though, because I kept talking to him, trying to interact. Obviously, he couldn't understand, but I could tell, in his head, he was playing army; in that moment, he was one of us. He didn't really understand what he had done or what was happening. All he knew is that he was with the invaders and it was the greatest thing that had ever happened to him. Nothing else mattered but his complete and total presence right then.

As the patrol kept moving throughout the morning and as light started to break on the day, I kept talking to him, just making conversation, idle chatter that he pretended to process for a moment then acknowledged with a smile. My men were getting more and more angry with me, though, like I was a traitor. I knew there was something wrong with him, but nobody else seemed to pick up on it. Or nobody else seemed to care. By daybreak, and as we finally arrived at a pre-designated checkpoint, I'd let him carry my pack for a little bit, eat a few snacks from my MRE, look through my night vision, and even hold my rifle for a minute. And I have never felt so good about anything I have ever done for a fellow human being.

At this point we'd gone much too far with him and with Higher. The wheels for the extraction of this guy were in motion, so I had to keep pretending we have an enemy captive in our midst. They could send an escort with the resupply choppers and we'd hand our detainee off to them for processing and interrogation. I could wash my hands of this whole debacle.

The birds were inbound and as they made their appearance on the horizon I pantomimed to this poor guy what was about to happen. He was ecstatic. The helicopter landed and the crew chief pushed out a few boxes filled with water, food, and batteries, and I handed off the detainee to a two-man escort in the back of the bird. And as the helicopter started to spin up again, getting ready to take our man back for interrogation, I looked back in the full light of morning and he and I made eye contact for the first time, like really looked into each other's eyes. I could tell he's having this moment of clarity, just as I was, an awakening. He was no longer smiling. He just stared at me, and I at him, until we were no longer able. We shared a moment of complete and utter stillness. In that moment I watched a young man give up everything he knew in exchange for the unknown otherness across a mystical border, a dream he had had since the early days of our invasion. I have watched my own children be born, but I have never felt like I felt right then, seeing a man's dream realized, lifted up and transformed in the back of a helicopter to his paradise, to freedom. This young man suspected there was something else, believed he was missing something, and he just wanted to find out what that something was.

By this point in the late morning, Jacuz is a madhouse, a circus freak show of soldiers and soon-to-arrive brass from all over the country as staffers begin to spread out over the rooftops. Trucks from my neighboring company can be heard breaching the outskirts of the northern part of the village. The elders are congregating again and want to know what is going on. But they already know. They most definitely know. But my boss acts as if I have never spoken to these men before and organizes a meeting with them at 1200. I have been awake now, more or less, little cat naps here and there, for a little more than twenty-eight hours, the long previous day bleeding into the night, the night bleeding into a new day. My boss has a steady supply of energy drinks he ensures are available wherever he goes. He is blowing and going, nonstop, excited to be off the sprawling support base that is Palermo. But we will not do anything new or inventive beyond search and clear every vehicle leaving and entering Jacuz. He will hold his meeting with the elders and try his best to make the most of a horrible situation. Updates stream in as the staff officers hug their notebooks, map markers, spreadsheets, print-outs of nebulous plans designed entirely on presentation programs originally designed, and much more useful, for businessmen in our nation to sell each other synergy or some other such corporate nonsense. The enlisted staff lackeys cling to radios and antennae and satellite linkups like toddlers with security blankets.

The additional company making their way into Jacuz is led by a friend and fellow company commander, a guy who will suddenly become the hero of the moment, a guy I like but who is my competitor and who has never lost a soldier and who has now been re-missioned in order to help support me and my men who have now given up a soldier to the enemy, though Alastor is still consider *Duty Status—Whereabouts Unknown*, or DUSTWUN, for ten days until he is designated MIA or the insurgency comes forward with evidence of him being a prisoner of war. Jacuz will now crawl with soldiers of my nation, a nation we all know and love, soldiers who are angry and pissed off and, knowing the glorious efficiencies of soldier internal communications firsthand, have already heard the rumor that Alastor left of his own accord.

What was Alastor thinking? Alastor was, and always has been, ever will be, along with those like him, even before his desertion, a mediocre soldier at best. I think you know this. You must know this as truth. He is a self-involved, *not-as-smart-as-he-thinks-he-is* product of a generation that thinks they are owed something. Anti-patriots. Traitors to a nation you and I love and cherish with our entire hearts.

"How's it going, Sergeant Major?"

"Could be better, sir."

Indeed. I do not have much to say to the sergeant major or to the first sergeant. Just awkward conversation. I move on quickly, self-consciously walking down the steps of the roof, my radioman dutifully following behind. But no one is watching. And no one cares.

"Hey, sir, the commander wants to see you again."

I turn to look at my radioman awaiting my response with a sarcastic smirk. I return a *what now* grimace and an eye roll and we head back up the steps to find the battalion commander pounding another energy drink, his naturally bugged and excitable eyes gaining rejuvenation with each deep glug.

"Alright, the colonel wants you pushed back to Chemera for initial statements and to refit. The S4 is taking the lead on the initial investigation. He'll be there later this afternoon. But I want you to push your guys. Get the statements and then we're sending you back out. What do you know about Gaumela?"

"Sir, I've been trying to get to Gaumela since we arrived in country. You know it's where we get rocketed from. But I'm not allowed according to the 3. Too risky. But there's definitely assholes in that town."

"Alright. We'll push you down there. Get down to the border and to Gaumela."

"So you want us in Gaumela now?"

"Don't be a smart ass. Yes, we want you in Gaumela. Predator picks up a lot of running around in there and we might just want to go test the waters. It's still your AO, Captain. I think you're the man with the right tactical know-how to stir things up down there and see if we get any sort of reaction."

"Yes, sir. Thank you, sir."

"Gather the boys, head back to Chemera, come up with a plan to probe the border, no clearing operations, just a patrol near—near. Captain—not on, not across, the border, see if that action will cause any sort of reaction. Know what I mean?"

"You mean a presence patrol, sir?"

"There's no such thing as presence patrol. You know that."

"Yes, sir."

"We both know Alastor isn't here nor in Gaumela. That poor kid is a hundred miles across the border in a safehouse. But we have to do what we have to do. The S3 has more details on constraints and escalation of force measures, declaring imminent threat, all the constraints. Get with him and then get out of here."

I start to turn to head back down off the roof, pleased that he confessed, at least to me, what we all know to be true.

"And Captain . . . I spoke to the first sergeant and the platoon leaders. We got ourselves a real nasty little situation here, don't we?"

"Yes, sir. I believe we do."

"Don't let it affect the men. Keep your soldiers busy and keep them focused. Keep. Them. Busy. You have a soldier missing. End of story."

"Yes, sir," and I head back down the steps again to tell the platoon leaders to start getting their men ready.

We now have clearance to go as close to the border as we want without crossing it, a border no one cares about but us. But we have laws in this time of war and I must abide by them. After a long twenty minutes with the S3, I gather my company and we begin the trek back to our home away from home at Chemera, a much longer walk than usual. The XO is waiting for us, gate open, hot chow ready when we finally arrive. I want to head straight for the barn and have a moment of peace and quiet to myself. But there is work to be done and we are sworn to do it. I head straight for the headquarters building and hunker down at my desk to start the plans process, a process I execute in a vacuum. This is a journey of discovery, of hopefulness, of pursuit, to which I have become addicted. I cherish this time.

15.

I HAVE BEEN THINKING of how to defeat the Gaumela problem since we first arrived at Chemera. What I came up with for this operation involves several teams infiltrating via foot under the cover of darkness through the rocky outcropping and hills surrounding the border village and then positioning these teams in strategic locations from which to best engage enemy forces. Once these elements are in position, we will bring in trucks via the main road to act as a decoy in hopes of attracting the enemy. The hope is that at least one of these hidden mountain positions would be able to engage and destroy said enemy when they expose themselves in an attempt to engage our trucks. This introduction of our mighty convoy of armored behemoths into the valley on the edge of Gaumela is the decisive point of our plan. The entire operation hinges on the enemy's reaction to this overt presentation. Yes, it is a simple patrol with trucks. This would appear to be a simple probing of the village with vehicles. We're not necessarily looking for a fight. But we will be ready in the mountain hide sites if fighters do show up.

Based on the drone feeds I have analyzed, and on satellite imagery provided to me, there are a series of what we call *rat lines*, or goat trails, through these mountains. The enemy uses these to move through the mountain passes undetected back and forth across the border. They will likely also use this same trail network to get into a position to fire on the trucks, thus exposing themselves to those of us in the hidden mountain ambush sites, at which time we will be allowed to fire on them, as they represent an imminent threat to the safety of our men in the valley. If the enemy is not in the mountains and has chosen to hide in the village or to actually attack from the village, well, our trucks can still defend themselves with superior firepower while those of us in the high ground move to support their withdrawal or, with approval from Higher, to clear the village. But if the enemy chooses to attack from the hills, as I believe they will, and down onto the trucks from across the border, then those of us in the hidden positions will close the loop and destroy the insurgents.

The safety of the men in the trucks is paramount. Some of the men feel they are being used as bait and are at a higher risk of fatality. To mitigate these effects on our mounted patrol, the plan calls for the trucks to be minimally manned, to still be able to return fire into the steep hills across the border, and to pull into the outskirts of the village and find a position which represents a difficult yet still enticing shot for an insurgent, one in which he would have to expose himself in order to get a decent shot. Additional instructions are for the men in the vehicles to remain buttoned up inside save for the gunners in the turrets. Our hope is that just the mere presence of the four vehicles in the vicinity will spur the insurgent defenders to take a few potshots, maybe a burst or two of fully-automatic machine gun fire, just enough to expose themselves to those of us pre-positioned on their flanks. We are admittedly also betting on the generally poor marksmanship of the insurgents. Finally, those of us in the three mountain hide sites hope to have eyes on any perpetrators well before they even take aim. The rules of warfare, in this war anyway, demand that *imminent threat by an enemy force* must be declared before we may fire across the border. Easy enough. And I must maintain this declaration, remain in direct contact with the enemy, in order to use my indirect fire assets or receive any close air support. Given these limitations, direct kills are optimal. Direct kills satisfy. Direct kills and we can all move on. So the moment the enemy is in a position in which they can fire on our vehicles, I will declare *imminent threat* and let the games begin before the enemy even gets a shot off.

As you may have already recognized, the plan relies upon the triangular nature of warfare: element A supports element B, creating an angle that will intersect element C and creates wholeness on the battlefield. All component parts of warfare must create these 180 degrees. This maxim begins with the very first rifleman whose own triangulated security bubble interlocks with the men to his left and right, creating a series of triangular tessellations until an entire area of operations is secure. All warfare operates in this trinity. And all warfare begins with the individual rifleman who sees the limits of his sector of fire as the limits of his existence, the limits of his natural earth and the place he inhabits in this moment. This is Military Science 101. It is not taught in any school.

Depending on the avenue of approach the enemy uses from across the border, our hope is that at least two of our positions will be able to engage the enemy. The plan will also call for the mortar section to come in behind us via foot under the cover of darkness with the rest of the dismounts in a position from which they can provide eighty-one-millimeter effects both directly on the target as well as in linear target patterns plotted to put effects on possible enemy egress routes. The addition of the mortars adds the necessary dimension required to elevate the fight to the next level of loop closure provided an extra layer of potential destruction that will ensure the loop stays closed.

This is a smoke-and-mirrors operation. I have briefed the S3 and spoken to the battalion commander, both of whom said *sounds great, good job, get after it*, or something to that effect. I know, though, that I and my company of men are, at best, a diversionary tactic, really nothing more. Alastor will not be rescued by us. My men and I are incapable of such operations. We know how to destroy. And *disrupt*. Lacking the ability to operate in a tactically surgical manner, we cannot rescue prisoners of war. Alastor could in fact be hidden away in Gaumela, but that is the least of my concerns. The more important matter at hand from my perspective involves letting the enemy that hides across this border and lobs rockets at me while I am peaceably trying to read my book about whaling know that the gloves are off. Like the private who only knows when his next guard shift starts and what time chow is served, the insurgents taking refuge in Gaumela only know that we have arrived to a place we have never been before. Let them think, or not think, what they will. Either way, they will fight all the harder and perhaps tip their own hand or shift assets to this border fight in the coming weeks allowing for a breakdown elsewhere in the country. I am in desperate need of a good fight. And we are *disrupting* them in this shell game.

A commander must position himself where he can best control the fight, best adjust his plan, and best shift and utilize assets across the battlefield. This is best from a tactical standpoint. Later, however, when he writes from this commander's vantage point, be it an hour, a week, a month, years later, his report will be tragically flawed.

You see, he has positioned himself to see the biggest possible picture. His account will fail to see the private on the distant hill that dropped his canteen and, having just untied it before the mission because he needed a little bit of 550 cord to hang up a makeshift poncho curtain next to his bunk and he honestly meant to replace the canteen tie-down but at some point was distracted by chow, or a game, or a work detail, and his squad leader did not re-check every single part of his soldier's uniform the day before an operation, having been on similar operations for eight months and having never had an issue before, then listening to said canteen tumble down the hill in the dark, a pinball machine on the side of a mountain setting off what sounds like an alpine avalanche, which then causes his entire squad to halt out of concern for *what in God's holy name is happening*, and then makes the point man lose his pace count and his compass bearing costing the squad fifteen minutes of time as this poor private, who has been so beaten about the head during his short time in the army that a soldier is never without six quarts of water, rather than leave the canteen, immediately chases after his tumbling canteen in the dark which luckily is jammed between two rocks and only found by guessing at the final resting place via echolocation and blindly grabbing in the dark thus causing the squad leader to significantly raise his pulse and now really feel the pressure to get to his position, so they move out quickly to make up time, and then the trail team leader, who cannot see so well with his night vision goggles, a problem he has always had but keeps to himself, and he does not see the faster pace until he is forced to speed up to twice the pace to keep up, and he twists an ankle, not badly but enough to smart under the weight of his pack, and the whole squad actually ends up in the wrong place well off of where they are supposed to be because the squad leader does not want to hold up the entire company so he reports that he is *in position* even though when the sun comes up he will not be able to see the objective, much less support the operation as he is tasked.

The commander will not get this version of events. And if he does get this version, in its entirety, he blames the squad leader for not ensuring his men's tie-downs are to standard up to and including the moments prior to stepping off on mission even though we all know a new private will do asinine things. But this account cannot make it into the commander's telling of the story for posterity as it shows either a lack of respect for his squad leaders and NCOs in general, an attempt to put the blame onto someone else, or a complete breakdown of discipline in his own ranks. At best, the retelling of such events comes across as self-aggrandizement of his unit, an attempt to make light of the foibles that befall us when men try to kill one another. None of which a good history makes.

What is written then is that *the squad struggles to get up the steep terrain in the pitch dark of the early morning, one man suffers a severe high ankle sprain yet the indomitable spirit of our nation's fighting men endures. The land navigation in these austere mountains is challenging, yes, but the point man finds a way, pressing on to the objective* and the reader is left to create a scenario in which he pictures rough men ready for battle inching up a mountain, step by agonizing step, to be in their prescribed place at the correct time in accordance with the operational template. History as poetry. But poetry is a lie we tell to insulate ourselves against reality. The truth is that a series of innocuous, altogether ridiculous events transpired, creating a ripple effect of shenanigans, some of which involve the breakdown of standards of conduct and discipline that go back to training in our home nation, and it is this, you must understand, that results in the dismantling and hamstringing of an entire operation. A private dropped his canteen on the movement to the overwatch position. A truth you will never know in the histories.

But, and go with me on this journey, it is still possible that the commander is never informed of the situation and the squad leader simply relays to the officer that the hill was steeper than initial analysis would suggest and the soldier's load was great. The leader himself remains unaware of the tiny events that take place—the dropped canteen, the twisted ankle, the flustered point man—that result in a mission not going as planned. But you must also understand that the poor private in our example does not feel the crushing weight of mission failure on his shoulders either. He is clueless. His vantage point is limited by what he sees around him, and he is unlikely to know what is taking place outside his own fire team, much less on the hill where a leader surveys his command and hopes to God the plan he worked so hard to create gets executed flawlessly. His events are his own. The private will recall them based on his relationship to the things over which he has power, just as the commander will do when he sits down to record events as he remembers them in an hour, a week, month, or years later. An inexperienced soldier dropped his canteen. This is the true history of our individual existence. This is the history we need but are never provided. This is the poetry of war.

16.

I AM SURE THAT in the last seventy-two hours nothing has changed in Jacuz save our nation's level of physical presence. Battalion headquarters has set up shop in the village. They are no longer my concern. The steady stream of resupply helicopters, with staffers and equipment coming and going, makes me feel sorry for the villagers. I am sure they just want to be left alone to tend their chickens and goats. There is only a cloud of dust surrounding Jacuz now, much like the cloud of dust the villagers continually saw surrounding Chemera just a few days prior with the regular arrival of resupply and transport helicopters and burn pit smoke. Now all they see are the clouds of dirt surrounding them. I am eager to get out of Chemera if for no other reason than to not have to see the distant storm, holding in place, enveloping Jacuz far across the desert floor.

0300. We start our walk to Gaumela. The five kilometers through the foothills and into the steep, rocky outcroppings that surround Gaumela is an arduous one, but largely uneventful. The half-moon sheds more light on our movement through the foothills than I would have preferred. But I did not get to vote on the timing of this operation.

I position myself in the squad hide site in which I can best see both what is happening in Gaumela as well as on the hilltop on the other side of the international border. The two other positions push into their sectors with some degree of effort, one on a slightly lower hilltop to my east, the other on higher, rockier ground to my west. The squad to my west, chosen to occupy this higher position as they have some of the fittest men in the company, struggles to get up the steep terrain in the pitch dark of the early morning, one man twists his ankle on the movement but they push on, arriving at their objective ready to work. The land navigation in these austere mountains is challenging, yes, but we all get to our prescribed positions just as the first rays of sunlight start to appear across the mountains.

And here we wait. We wait in the silence of the cool, still morning. We wait, watch, and pray in the mystery of our own presence. In the back of my mind, in the simplest recesses of my subconscious, I want to see a thick line drawn in the mountains that divide these countries, a border delineating good from bad, right from wrong. But here, all is one. There is only a single all-encompassing beauty in these mountains, the deepest sense of the supernatural burrowing deep under my skin and forcing a reckoning with my job and the task at hand. How can a place so perfect in every aspect of physical existence be so ignorant of our purpose here, of our desire to help and to make life even better in this tiny corner of creation? We settle in and watch, waiting for the arrival of our trucks, our mythic decoys, and hope these cowardly insurgents, hiding behind a border no one here truly cares about, make their presence known.

The fight here is one of long distance and we have armed ourselves accordingly. By cross-leveling across the company, we have managed to get each position two M14 enhanced battle rifles for precision fire on the target. I carry one myself, equipped with scope and all the accessories for long-range precision marksmanship. If we fail in a direct fire engagement, we have two eighty-one-millimeter mortar tubes ready for action. And if we still do not destroy them directly, my plan is for the eighty-ones in conjunction with our M240 machine guns to create enough of a wall to pin them down until the Apaches or other close air support arrives.

Still, we wait, held to the ground by the rays of a glorious sunrise, the morning exploding on the mountain horizon like a bomb released in slow motion from beneath the earth's crust. The light glides in, enveloping our world, inching skyward as we sit in our hide sites only occasionally sitting up behind a rock in hopes of just a tinge of relief for numb limbs and aching knees. I wonder if the soldiers in the other positions feel the earth moving beneath them. I wonder if the men lying in the dirt and rocks around me now sense the unity with the universe the way I do.

0842. The trucks rumble in the distance and my heart races. Let's do this. Ten minutes later and the trucks are still just rumbles in the distance, the grinding slog of giant steal beasts laboring across an inhospitable landscape. The rise and fall of the engine noise as they crawl across the terrain keeps time with our anxious heartbeats. Finally, the first truck comes into view as she rounds the rocky corner of the mountain road and maneuvers into the boulder-strewn valley just outside the village. A manmade atrocity she is, a magnificently invented beast, a testament to our prowess and will to survive on a planet indifferent to our desire for power—a seething, crawling contradiction on wheels. The lone, all-seeing, and powerful soldier in the copula spins and turns and scans his sector, having resigned himself to his fate atop the churning, agile behemoth, breathing the exhaust fumes deep into his lungs with each sway of the vehicle upon the rough road pulling him towards Gaumela.

The first truck finds a tailor-made position tucked into a small depression as two more of our still-new, sixteen-ton M-ATVs find their place, instinctually creating a herringbone formation. Not bad. Good spread. Protected. Menacing yet somehow just vulnerable enough from this vantage point. Finally, the tail of our convoy, an older model MAXXPro rounds the corner and, seeing no place to tuck into, eases back toward the rock outcropping to cover the backside of the convoy. Beautiful. I have not said a word over the radio. This is the poetry we all want in our history.

And we wait.

Military life is an existence filled to overflowing with waiting. Often times the waiting is for nothing of significance: a series of shots and vaccinations, mountains of paperwork to be filled out and signed, waiting to draw the latest gear a defense contractor has duped our nation into buying, chow. But despite all our complaints about waiting in the military, the truth of the matter is that all of this waiting has prepared us for what happens at the end of the line. Our military lives are not an endless parade of joys, thrills, gratification, and self-satisfaction. Military life, and the wars associated with such life, represents an endless parade of menial work conducted for poor pay with little to no immediately observable dividends in hopes that one day all our waiting, all our struggles, both our physically demanding work and the simple, mind-numbing, soul-crushing tedium that makes up the bulk of our days will pay off in the end. Our army, an army I love and cherish, created a system of continuous pursuit in which the happiness lies in the journey. No one has guaranteed me that the enemy will make themselves known this morning, that they will crop up on the hill, rocket-propelled grenades on shoulders, machine guns slung, ammo belts wrapped around their shoulders, and give me the glorious fight I so desire right now. I am not promised an end state but rather only that I can wait, work, wait, repeat. War makes no promises save the constant searching for fleeting, transitory moments.

Today, however, luck is on our side. As if on cue, the first enemy soldier crests the far hill with a jaunty *I'm-about-to-rain-down-death* step and begins his descent down the steep hillside at a range of roughly one kilometer. He has a weapon, but even with my optics I cannot quite make out exactly what it is while he is on the move. Small arm, but not an AK. Looks bolt action. The RPG, along with the ubiquitous PKM light machine gun, arrive moments later with the second and third men over the hill, the same joyous expediency in their movements, slipping and sliding down the steep embankment. My position has the best bead on the insurgents. Funny how that works. Now it is only a matter of what angle the enemy takes to engage the trucks as to how effective our plan will be. We watch and we hope. The enemy, all together now, slip out of sight behind one of the many false crests and micro-valley undulations in these foothills. There are two places they could show themselves again, an easy shot roughly five hundred yards away and a position offering better coverage two hundred yards closer but at an odd angle down into the valley. Let us hope for the farther but more exposed shot.

A head pops up behind a rock, a blur at first, hallucinatory, and it takes a few seconds to confirm that it is indeed a man. All I have to do is declare *imminent threat*, declare that these men are about to fire on us, and they are mine. But I do not want to say the words—an *international law of land warfare check-the-box-and-save-your-ass declaration*—until I am sure I can put the first one down and the rest of my men can go to work on the remainders. He will have to pop up on the rock and expose his full body in order to get a clean shot, both for himself and for me. All three men are still well protected from the trucks. A good position for them to be in from their perspective. An even better position from our perspective. They take turns peeking over and around rocks, trying to decide which of our trucks to engage.

"Call Battalion, Junior. Tell them we have imminent threat from a three to five-man enemy element."

I set myself up for a seated five-hundred-yard shot, rifle nestled in a small crook between two boulders. I prefer a light, floating, tip-of-the-finger trigger pull that slowly drags through the trigger guard as I clear my head of all superfluities, all extraneous thoughts, cutting out the garbage until I blank out, drift away in a bubble as if . . .

. . . speaking to an elderly parent, one that will remember events that never actually happened: movies watched, school plays attended, details of a long-ago family vacation or a distant family squabble. These are verifiable events that can be looked up. I can easily research when a certain movie came out or dig through an old scrapbook to show the dates of a school play, or playoff game, or rifle through the family photos to show I was or was not at an event in question. These are verifiable events on a universal timeline that demonstrate a flawed memory. *We cannot have seen that movie together as I had already moved out of the small home where we kept chickens and a small vegetable garden and was already a soldier in our nation's army* is what *needs* to be said. But it is not. Nothing is said. A combination of pity, childhood fear, and respect prevents us from ruining the moment in the parent's mind, a protective bubble we have built around our parent's psyche. Why torture them? What is to be gained? A flawed history is not flawed to its believer. A flawed history only props up the believer's understanding of reality. I suffer not one iota by letting the parent go on with their false memories. The truth is mine and mine alone because one day I too hope to be elderly. And I want my memories to be calm and sure, complete in their own existence.

. . . Inhale, exhale. Slowly. That's it. Slink and slither up onto that rock, you border-hugging, power-craved, resentful piece of human trash . . . relax . . . feel your trigger finger at rest . . . feel the memory you are about to create for me . . .

And goddammit all to hell if I will let someone alter my future stories based on pesky dates and times and impossibilities. This is my poetry, my history, a perfect nest of thought and memory. You have yours. Leave mine alone. So when I look through the scope of my rifle and prepare to pull the trigger, to create a blip on the eternal loop for the glory of our nation's foreign policy, I wonder, when I am old and telling my grandchildren about my days as a war fighter, how best to remember this man who has crossed a border he does not recognize and who I am about to rescue from his own future, and his own flawed memories of today's events.

. . . In . . . out . . . natural pause . . . squeeze . . . recoil . . .

The pursuit complete. The insurgency plays directly into the warrior's hand. Now let us sit back and watch the game play out as it has for generations. This is our story now. My travels on the loop remembered the way I wish you to remember them. The way I relay the facts to you. You are not here. Not now. Not in this moment. This is a moment between me and the man on that rock dying for his cause.

The air is clear and pure and as real as the insurgent that just collapsed in my sight-picture. My duty complete. This most basic function of warfare is never as dramatic as you might think. But dammit if sometimes a target of opportunity does not present itself and we must act accordingly to create our snapshots of history, blips on the Möbius strip of our generation's war. A club, a battle axe, a broad sword, a cannonball, or 7.62 in the chest: it matters not. The enemy slumps, folds in half, removed from the loop.

I turn my attention to the men with me in this mountain hide site who have already opened fire on my cue, unleashed hell, if you will, blanketing the hillside in a rich cone of fire as the enemy dances, twists, and ricochets from rock to rock, whirling holy men on a quest for nirvana. I hear the first *thumps* of eighty-one-millimeter and wait for the splash of rounds that will cover the hillside momentarily. Another insurgent hit, a dirty sheet lying on the side of his rocky home. I weaken. The clarity that strikes all fighting men rears its ugly head. *I wonder if the man upon which I just executed my sacred duty liked chickens? If he liked to tuck their heads under his arm and stroke their soft feathers, thinking pensively about his life, such as it is, tucked away*

in these mountains, such as they are? I wonder where his goats are right now?
Such moments must be pushed down deep inside.

Pulling myself out of this dangerous thought I watch my men, now free to open fire, gleeful, alive, firing aimless shot after shot, and I wonder if they too are thinking about their elderly parents' flawed memories or about the chickens the men they are attempting to destroy may like to keep. Are they thinking about how they will remember the man they shot and the concept of memory itself, of what memories are flawed and what memories are outright lies we tell ourselves to stay alive until we are old and no one dares to correct our memories out of respect? Did the enemy tumble, topple, dive, dance, collapse, or did he arch his back dramatically, then fall forward as if on a flimsy saloon balcony from which he must then do a half-flip in order to land on his back in a water trough conveniently located directly beneath him? However death occurs, the scene changes each time we tell the story, each time we are called upon to unfold a little of our history.

"Cease fire. Cease fire. Cease fire."

The majestic mountains ring with the final reverberations of our nation's power and might. They never knew what hit them. We can pack up and move back to Chemera. Mission accomplished. *Disrupted.*

"Tell Battalion threat neutralized. We had a small engagement. Nobody hurt. End of story."

"Yes, sir. Exactly like that?"

"Sassy it up in report format, Junior. I'll backbrief the S3 when we get back to Chemera."

"Got it."

There is no reason to report the enemy deaths. Not yet anyway. I know they are dead. You now know they are dead. And that is all anyone ever need know.

The walk back is uneventful, high-spirited, and quick. The men are pleased with their work, and I allow them this moment of celebratory reflection unique to the soldier and his work. The opportunity to fire your weapon with impunity, to have ambushed an enemy who has harassed you from behind a border these many months now, to define success on the terms you established, is satisfying. Whatever it takes, for whatever reason, I like to see the men happy. I know events did not go as briefed and as planned. This is fact. But I prefer not to delve into the truth. All that needs to be known, by you and anyone else, is that each element was in their exact prescribed position. Men on a great whaling ship, fulfilling their contractual obligations to a grateful captain and, more importantly, a grateful nation, a nation likely to never hear of such planned actions, actions taking place daily on a continual basis for countless years, on an international border straddling two countries, one country at war with an insurgency and one pretending to not be supportive of that insurgency. Two, possibly three, enemy soldiers left to die on a rocky hillside, straddling a border between good and evil.

And as we stride into Chemera, walking on air, feeling alive and renewed in this smallest of victories, putting a few *insurgents* out of their misery by allowing them to die for their cause, I am greeted by a major I do not know, his staff lieutenant, and a master sergeant.

"Captain, we need to talk."

17.

I DID NOT SIMPLY give up my imaginary baseball game after my first combat experiences. I continued to try and play the game. The game, however, became an impossibility, and it had to be freed. In attempts to play the game post-combat, I became too much like the men being created. The game was no longer in the margins, insomuch as it ever was, but rather occupied a wholeness in me, transporting me down onto the field instead of allowing me to remain the distant and aloof analytic statistician in the stands, viewing the geometry and tessellation of what used to be our nation's national pastime from afar. What was once a game of statistical analysis was now real, the numbers digging deep into my soul, and I was unable to escape the heightened sense of nature I now felt all around me.

In my youth and into my pre-combat adulthood, when playing my imaginary game I was also able to actively play the game in various youth and, later, adult teams and leagues with a fair amount of skill while still maintaining the ability to separate the two activities. At least, I thought I kept the two activities separate. The fact of the matter, in hindsight, is that these two critical components of my youthful formation were battling each other each time I engaged exclusively in one or the other. Because, as you might have guessed, and as hard as it is for me to admit to you, my actual gameplay had significant flaws which I now know manifested themselves on paper in my imaginary games. Despite a pretty swing, my bat was in fact slow, and, as is the case for most lefties with pretty swings and slow bats, I tended to pull everything. This slow bat coupled with my crippling fear of striking out further forced me to feel the need to swing at everything even remotely close to the plate. And despite being a slick-fielding outfielder, my throwing arm was weak. This weak arm did not bode well for me on the occasions when I would be called to the mound to pitch: a beautiful delivery, flawless in form, nothing but strikes—fat strikes, right down the middle of the plate strikes, served up like they were on a tee.

This, then, was the way of my imaginary game, a statistical dreamscape in which flaws were overcome in order to achieve success, the creation of a world in which I could participate and be successful of my own accord. Alone, unafraid, unbuoyed by the realities of my natural circumstances. My made-up players were always left-handed. The stadiums in which they played always had a short right-field fence. I now know that my players were me, transported to a playing field in which they could be happy and success-ful working for the simple sake of work and thriving off their own natural abilities, the abilities that were bestowed upon them and for which they were free to practice of their own will by their own measure of success. I was creating a world of my own isolation, a world in which I could abandon the trappings of expectations and the realities of on-field failures.

So when my eyes were opened up to the world of combat and I began to see the world differently, I lacked the ability to keep these worlds separate. All life merged and there was no longer any desire to create a world outside of my realities. Combat was real. Everything else would be measured against that yardstick of physical reality on an eternal loop of event recurrence. Even in retelling this to you, dear reader, I know a transfiguration always took place that was either subconsciously ignored or was in fact completely set aside in order to function in a world in which I felt I was living out a great divorce of two competing realms of existence. My games were played on a border, in the marginalia, in an attempt to create new realities out of the tedium, boredom, or unfulfilling nature of what I faced in a world over which I had no control. But all that is out the window once you have fought in combat for your country, a country you love dearly. All that is out the window once you have tasted all that is real in the cosmos.

Seeing this major, now standing here in front of me, takes the wind out of my sails. I know why he is here. The rest of our nation's army continues to do great work in the search for Alastor, though we all know the truth. My authorization to stir things up in Gaumela was only to keep me and my men busy and focused on other matters so that the investigation could continue unabated by any contrivances on our part. But here we are post-mission, back at Chemera. I had, for the moment, forgotten why I was allowed to push to the border to begin with. That this is all for Alastor. The circum-stances of a soldier's disappearance must be investigated, analyzed, parsed apart, decisions made and answers provided to a nation and to a family. The command climate and culture of my company must be examined. My tactics, decision-making process, counseling of subordinates, and training methods must be picked apart and evaluated for no other reason than to find a scapegoat for what has happened. Someone must be blamed.

"What's up, sir? Investigative team?" I ask.

"You got it."

"Let me put my gear up and grab some chow. I assume the XO has taken care of you?"

"Yep."

"Then I'll meet you back in the CP in about thirty minutes?"

"I still have some reports I can work on, so take your time. Make it an hour. I'll be with the first sergeant."

"Works for me, sir."

I hate him already. And his sycophants. But they have a job to do, and there is no sense in getting on their bad side. I am sure he is not exactly thrilled to be given this tasking. A tasking for which he is likely on the bottom rung of a very tall ladder. I will be compelled to make another statement, my second of the ordeal, having already provided a brief statement to our own S4 when we first came back to Chemera. Those statements will likely go in a folder that will be added to a growing stack of folders full of findings and observations and analysis and non-disclosure agreements of what might have happened. The first steps in a long march to ascertain what is an inconvenient truth.

I swing through the mess tent and pick up a slice of stale coffee cake to take back to my room.

"Today was awesome, sir," a team leader from Second Platoon tells me as I police up the sweetest cake-topping crumbles from the tray with my thumb.

"Hell yeah, it was."

I feel good that I made this soldier happy if even for a moment, providing him a connection to reality and hopefully made him realize his purpose on the earth, the reason he joined his nation's military to begin with: to destroy the enemies of our nation in armed combat. He got to do that today. And I am proud of him.

I deflect several more such brief comments on the day's operation, the men still on a high that will soon fade once they climb into their dank squad buildings and put on a bad movie, sit silently in the dark for hours on end, numb once again to their real potential and purpose. Once back in my room I neatly arrange my gear the way I always do, every piece of equipment in its proper place, sit down on my cot, make some notes in my journal about today's operation, and read a page from my book on whaling while munching on the stale cake. I do not keep track of where I am in the book, preferring to just pick up and begin reading at any point in the narrative. I find there is no steady progress to be found in a book about whaling. There is no need to go through fixed portals of narrative structure in order to reach an end state. The story just is. At any point. Until it is not.

I get up off my cot after reading a single page, resisting the urge for a nap, and with still twenty or so minutes left before I must meet the investigating major, walk down to the aid station for a cold water from the medic's refrigerator. Walking by the main CP door, I hear the major and his two flunkies in conversation with the first sergeant. He will keep them occupied for some time. It is obvious the major has rarely left his compound, wherever it may be, and is excited to be part of something big, eager to lap up the first sergeant's war stories for the time being.

The aid station is unoccupied and I immediately spot Alastor's personal belongings in the corner, boxed up several days ago, ready to go back with the investigator. Two duffel bags full of gear, a mostly empty rucksack, and a cardboard box full of books and letters and assorted snacks and sundry items. I grab a water from the fridge and, against my better judgment, walk over to the stack of Alastor's gear to rifle through his stuff. I am telling myself now, as I am telling you, that this action is just to get a better sense of who this kid is. Nothing more. And this is the truth as I see it.

On top of all his gear is a stack of letters from home and a couple of books: a poetry collection about love and nature and a war book about a man who survives a heavy bombing by our own nation when he was a prisoner of war in a war fought by a previous generation of soldiers. I have read this book before. It is an important book for soldiers to read *after* they have experienced combat but is completely useless beforehand. The story makes no sense if one has never experienced combat, such as it is. I find it interesting that Alastor was reading this book.

Atop this stack of reading material is a leather-bound journal. I would not typically read a man's journal. Sacrosanct territory. A man's innermost thoughts and aspirations are not to be trifled with or delved into without express permission. The vast majority of men do not keep journals anyhow. This is their loss. A journal is the opposite of a burn pit. It is a man's internal crypt dug to his exact specifications and with no residual smell or smoky, polluting haze to filter truth. This is the reality in which we seek to hide ourselves, ideas burned at the altar of the pen, engraved in our hearts and minds, our personal detritus kept hidden in a book until we, serving as our own archeologist and our own judge of truth, revisit our words and decide what is fact and what is fiction. Nothing is hidden, everything is saved. Not consumed but created. My own maintenance of a personal journal has been spotty at best throughout my life and there is only one reason I can give for this failure on my part: fear of getting caught keeping a journal.

But the situation now is anything but typical. I convince myself to steal a glance at Alastor's writing so that I, his long-suffering commander, might find a piece of useful information towards solving the riddle that is Private First Class Alastor. I am not now, standing here in the aid station, afforded the luxury of sitting and reading the journal in its entirety. I can hear the first sergeant and the major across the hall in the big command room and know that they will likely still be at least a few minutes more. But I do not want to get caught reading this kid's journal any more than I want to get caught keeping my own journal. I just want to flip around and see what I can see, read what Alastor records, feel what Alastor feels, if even for a moment, just to be in what was once his presence.

18.

I UNWRAP THE LEATHER string wrapped around the journal and start near the beginning, a decent enough place to start:

Sep 3rd. We arrive to our final destination, Combat Outpost Chemera I think it's called, five days ago. We spent my first two weeks in country at Camp Palermo and most of the time I have been on a detail of some sort: ammo detail, trash detail, range police, guard duty, it never ends. I missed a lot of supposed mandatory training because my team leader puts me on every detail. He is an incompetent asshole who never tells me anything then will make me do push-ups until I can't do anymore or low crawl ungodly distances. Everyone knows he's an asshole but nobody messes with him. This is his first combat deployment, just like mine, but you'd think he was a war hero already. He went to some pretty tough schools and has all the cool uniform badges and he's in really good shape so everybody worships him. I'm in good shape too, but apparently it's the wrong kind of shape. I'm the fastest guy in my platoon but nobody cares about that. It's how many push-ups you can do that matters. Half these jerks don't even go all the way down when they do a push-up. But whatever.

I spent the last two weeks without my journal or books or even headphones as I wasn't told our duffel bags would be put away and we'd be living out of our rucksacks while at Palermo. I'm writing this now under my flashlight and fully inside my sleeping bag. They make fun of me for writing in a journal and won't let me use my flashlight to write because they say it bothers them while they're watching movies. That's all they do. Watch movies . . . mostly porn. Every night. I'm not sure another soldier in my squad, maybe even the company, even brought a book. I take that back, I have seen the officers with books, so I guess someone else in the company reads. But they read boring military histories and biographies, so it doesn't count. I saw some guys with comic books too . . . but that doesn't count either.

Just like Palermo, ever since we got here at Chermera (I'm not sure how to spell it) I've been on detail, and this is really the first chance I've had to write anything. There is a rumor going around that we will start patrols in the next day or two but my team leader hasn't said anything yet. I also heard our mid-tour leaves were cancelled because the fighting season will start in early spring and it's supposed to be a big one and we're doing a surge for the whole deployment. I really don't care because I'm here and it's just easier to stay rather than go back and have to then come all the way back over again. We haven't heard anything about mail yet but there were boxes of stuff left behind by the last unit that was here. Mostly cheap socks, crushed and melted snacks, and letters from schoolchildren. It made me feel really bad that these things went unopened and unused. I started reading the letters when I was on detail to clean out a big shed behind the main building but my team leader called me a fag and told me to keep working. I nabbed some socks instead but I can't really wear them since they're all cotton. And white. Maybe I can find another use for them.

Sep 27th. I really hate that I'm not able to write more. But it's hard to find a place to write in my journal. Right now, I'm in a tower pulling my guard shift. It's 0230. My buddy and I work out a deal though where he sleeps for an hour while I watch and then we switch off. I should be scanning the area now in my night vision goggles, but really I don't see the point. I take a look around every once in a while, but it is pitch black out there, and even with night vision I just see an empty green haze. Every rock looks like a person sneaking up on the compound. But even if there were a single person, or even two or three, what will they do? Explode themselves at the wall? It would take a large element to actually storm the outpost. And we'd see them coming. So I write in my journal. Finally.

We've been on a few patrols but nothing has really happened yet. We walk to the village and then I pull guard along a mud wall for six hours and then we come back. I'm excited for something to happen but also don't want bad things to happen. Just, anything would be nice.

The people here seem to not care that we're even here. I guess they've seen it all before and we all look the same to them anyway. The kids just run up to us while we're pulling guard and beg for candy. I usually give them all of my candy, and I was even able to bring an extra MRE one time and pass it out. Some of the guys like to give the kids rations that they know the child's religion will not allow them to eat. They can't read the packaging so they don't know that the food in the package is forbidden. I tell the guys that this is messed up and they mostly tell me to shut the fuck up.

I'm probably the most hated guy in our platoon. I'm not entirely sure why this is, and I don't really care. I hate these guys too. I joined the army for all the right reasons—duty, honor, country—but am made fun of relentlessly for ever mentioning these reasons. Apparently, the only reason any one can have for joining the military is a desire to kill people. I get that on a barbaric level, but I also need the comfort of knowing that there is a reason for the conduct of my duty, that my killing is part of the duty, honor, country I joined for. Most of these guys don't care why they're here or what the people over here think or how they live their lives, they just want to do bad things to those they have labeled bad people. I don't necessarily see these people as bad, nor backward, in any threatening sense of the words. Some of them seem good to me, from what I can tell. The children always seem to be smiling. I believe we can help these people escape the grip of the rulers we are ousting that controlled their culture with an iron fist. I believe we're here for the right reasons, but being around my fellow soldiers so much, I'm beginning to forget what those reasons are.

Sep 30th. We got rocketed this evening right before stand-to! Nobody was hurt, but a rocket messed up one of our trucks. Someone said the rockets came from across the border. Which makes sense. We are in the middle of a big open expanse of desert. There are mountains on three sides of us off in the distance and nobody understands why we're here. We're a long walk (an hour at least) from the closest village, and there are enough small hills and big rock outcroppings close enough to us for the enemy to rocket us and then sneak back across the border. It would make more sense to either put us directly on the border, on the top of a mountain, or further out into the desert highlands so that the enemy would at least have to expose himself if we wanted to attack the base with rockets.

I share a tiny hut with seven other soldiers, all crammed into a smelly, overcrowded room with no windows and a single door. As the lowest ranking man in the squad, I am stuffed into the far back corner where I am subjected to every smell, every naked ass, every swinging dick, in the room.

I asked the room one time right before lights out if maybe everybody could take a break from their porn. It seems like a reasonable question to me but the reply was a resounding *fuck you, Alastor.* They seem to think that if they are covered in their sleeping bags, I don't know that they're playing with themselves and then getting up in the middle of the night to jerk off into the shit buckets. My team leader suggested that I'm a closet queer, though, and that all these naked men in the room were turning me on. This makes zero sense, but it got a big laugh.

I spend as much time as I can in my books. This is how I pass my days.

I begin to feel bad for Alastor after only thumbing through these entries, maybe even feeling a bit of the kindred spirit in him I detected at the one interaction we shared at the range back in our home country. But these journal entries were early ones, and anyone, especially young and vulnerable privates, will have some doubts about their place in the overall scheme of events. Most people will settle in to the routine and adapt to the combat environment. These are just musings of a lost and bored kid. And Alastor is clearly not resilient. He may very well be the most hated man in the platoon, though I have found in my military career that such labels come and go with each new influx of privates or one bad mistake by a junior leader. I do know his team leader, though. And he *is* an ass-kissing piece of shit. I flip ahead:

Dec 15th. I am very much in a routine now. Rocketed in the morning, patrol during the day, guard duty at night, repeat. Nothing changes. I actually like going out on patrol because it gets me away from the smell of the burn pit and out of that nasty-ass room for the day. I got some letters from my parents and that made me feel good. I've been writing them pretty regularly and they both support me over here, so that's good. I didn't tell them about the three firefights I've been in as I didn't want to worry them. If I said we were in a fight, they will picture an elaborate war movie, and it just wasn't like that. I haven't even fired my weapon yet, though the other guys go ballistic as soon as they hear shots from anywhere. My buddy emptied an entire 30-round magazine into an orchard for no reason after we heard three rounds faintly in the distance. He wasn't alone of course.

I don't blame the guys. I want some heavy action, too. They just seem to take things too far. I also know to be careful what you wish for. Maybe the fights we've been in are enough. The older guys talk about how it was on their other deployments. Everyone has stories from the last time they were here but nothing from now. The rockets have injured a few guys with shrapnel, just minor injuries, though, so we've been lucky in that regard. I'd hate to go out that way. A rocket out of nowhere. I at least want a fighting chance if I get taken out.

I sometimes forget what it was like to be a private, to have joined the military of our nation with all the propaganda baggage that comes with re-cruitment and initial training, then wading through all the bullshit to arrive at some semblance of this way of doing things, some sort of coping mecha-nism to make this new life tenable. The trick as a new soldier, though, if you intend to have any sort of success in this line of work, is to realize you were largely duped, and from that point create your own reality, invent a soldier's life in your head that will reconcile propaganda with truth. You must find a way to combine these two lives: a life of fact and a life of fiction into a new existence. Otherwise, you will go nuts. The best soldiers figure this out early in their careers. The ones who don't get out at the first opportunity. Maybe I have that backward.

I flip to a really long entry from the day we did a company picnic and what amounts to a day off of patrols in appreciation for all the hard work the soldiers do and in remembrance of a holiday we celebrate back in our home nation. The day is meant for the soldiers to relax a little bit, to grill some steaks we fly in special from Camp Palermo, maybe play some volleyball or touch football, and then do a little show with skits and whatever else the guys want to perform: no details, minimal guard duties, no patrols. But I suppose not everyone ends up enjoying these activities as much as intended:

Dec 25th. We didn't do any patrolling today and the cooks ac-tually cooked up a pretty decent meal with grilled steaks and potatoes and cake. I don't know if it was actually good or if it just seemed good because we eat so many MREs and usually have the same thing for breakfast and dinner. Had a sort of company barbecue, I guess you'd call it. Sports and just laying around do-ing nothing. In the evening the first sergeant said we would do company skits, make fun of the chain of command, make fun of each other, whatever we wanted . . . total immunity. A spotlight was set up on the backside of the big storage barn to light up what served as the stage area. It sounds silly, I know, but I was actually looking forward to the skits, and I had a good time, un-til the very end, when Team Leader Dickhead made me get up in front of everyone just to ridicule me. Most of the guys were doing songs from home and singing tunes they liked when they were kids just a few years ago. Some of the guys told jokes and ragged on each other. They made fun of the commander and the first sergeant and how they don't seem to really get along, like a husband and wife that have been together for a real long time and now just get on each other's nerves. All that was really fun. But after all the skits were done and people were starting to leave and head back to their squad huts, my team leader ordered me up on stage to recite the poetry he somehow knew I had been reading and memorizing. I think the piece of shit has been reading my journal. So he knows I already hate him. Do you hear that, Sergeant? I do not like you, and you do not like me.

I tried to get out of taking the stage and even now as I write this, in the guard tower, I regret doing as he said. I should have refused. It would have been easier on me if he just made me low crawl or do push-ups as punishment rather than reciting poetry to the smattering of guys still hanging around. I didn't want to recite poetry to these shits. But I am weak and I gave in.

When I finally relented, I told myself that I would not dumb myself down for anyone. This was me. And not everyone is like this ass-bag of a team leader (I hope you're reading this, Sergeant) nor do they want to be. I know in my heart that there are others here who joined for the same reasons I did, have the same feelings as me, do not want to just watch movies all night and who believe in something bigger than themselves. But they're scared. They're pandering to this buffoon and all the buffoons like him and we all get brought down to his level. But I refuse to change who I am and what I believe. So I took a deep breath and announced: "These are the last eight lines from one of my favorite poems. It's by a man who lived in the old country a long time ago:

> It is a woe too deep for tears, when all
> Is reft at once, when some surpassing Spirit,
> Whose light adorned the world around it, leaves
> Those who remain behind, not sobs or groans,
> The passionate tumult of a clinging hope;
> But pale despair and cold tranquility,
> Nature's vast frame, the web of human things,
> Birth and the grave, that are not as they were."

Alastor has placed the poem excerpt, the excerpt he recited, on a separate page, all to itself, in suddenly impeccable handwriting, alone and unafraid, as if the words were written specifically for me. I am touched by his choice of poem, pleased somehow that he has placed these words on a separate page, as if he clearly understood that these words are holy.

I know exactly what this poem means. Not that I believe poems have specific universal meanings per se but rather that a poem must speak to you first in a general sense of aesthetic beauty and then we may dig into its deeper meaning. The true meaning of a poem lies within the rapturous sense of romantic beauty felt upon a first reading. Clarity be damned. The poem is as real as the reader feels. A physical manifestation of life written to scale as seen from above. From that initial guttural analysis further elucidation on the deeper meaning of the verse might be found when we are compelled to read the piece again and again. But it is the initial beauty of this created reality that draws us in to find individual meaning, not unlike the sensation experienced when reading my book on whaling. True meaning and purpose arrive in waves on the page. Just when I think a passage or an entire chapter is understood, I find myself in another daydream or completely lost to the action yet still clinging to the side of the ship seeking truth in the words. Then the realization suddenly strikes that I do not have to understand what is happening. Reality just happens. Truth, facts, knowledge be damned. The simple enjoyment of life is all that matters. The rest is a web of lies and deceit, not as they seem. And we are alone . . . to brood, to wax poetic, to live in the fullness of our time. What this young private, a soldier in service to our great nation, a nation we all know and love, recited on the night of the Company Organizational Day and then wrote about in his journal I understand clearer than any orders I have ever been handed by Higher, took to heart deeper than any correction a parent or a teacher ever made to me, and felt in the depths of my soul beyond the limits of any admonition given by a boss:

Birth and the grave, that are not as they were.

Time closes around me, tightening my skin, squeezing my veins. Reading the journal elicits a panic within, a need to read the entire thoughts and feeling of this soldier, but I cannot, not yet. *Get through as much of it as you can*, I think to myself. I push on completely confident in the knowledge of what will happen next:

I never want to forgot how I felt that night. When I was done reciting: silence. Everyone wasn't exactly staring at me but they weren't not staring at me either. They were frozen in time, waiting for a reaction from my team leader—the fit guy, the loudmouth, the insecure bully. He laughed. Loud. And then he screamed: "Why me? Why did I get the fucking weirdo?" Everyone joined him in laughter, but I know deep down inside that at least a few of the guys were really interested in the poem and respected me for reciting it. It's not possible that I am that much different from everyone else. I don't understand why just a few idiots screw things up for the rest of us. And why so many soldiers lack the guts to stand up to these morons. It's not like I didn't know what these guys were like before we deployed over here, though. Maybe it is my fault. It's not as if I just materialized here, at Chemera, with no foreknowledge of the men I'd be living and working with. I'd spent an entire year since my basic training getting to know them and training with them and getting ready for this. So I know that a typical Friday night for my peers consists of getting drunk, going to strip clubs, starting fights with the sad, middle-aged locals who go to these clubs, hitting on women, striking out with women, coming back to the barracks pissed off only to get more drunk and fight in the hallways until they pass out. I was harassed relentlessly during these Friday-night excursions as my roommate was one of the ringleaders in this cycle of shame and disgust. I sat in my room and read, happy to have the place to myself for at least the six or seven hours they were gone and then being abruptly woken by the sounds of yelling, screaming, maniacal laughter, and broken bottles. My roommate would stumble into the room, last week's cut above his eye reopened and bleeding onto his stretched and ripped shirt from the attempt some other drunkard in the hallway made to choke him out. He'd stumble in and turn on the giant stereo, completely indifferent to my existence. I should not then be surprised that this would be my way of life here in Chemera, the pent-up anger and frustration made worse by the lack of alcoholic outlet—though I suspect many of my peers are having alcohol sent to them in containers of mouthwash—and all of us crammed together in a tiny room, only going out to actual work, on actual mission, six to eight hours a day three to five times a week. Between patrols? Guard duty, trash and shit burning details, ammo details, etc. Many of us never get to use the makeshift gym, take a walk around the fort—small as it is, a leisurely stroll on my own would do wonders for my mental stability—or just sit in the mess tent and relax for a few minutes. I go on patrol, and, if I'm not on detail, I'm forced to sit in a room with these assholes. I hate them. And I don't want to hate them. In my highest ideals, this was all for duty, honor, and country. But even at the most basic of levels, setting aside the high ideals I have ascribed to the military and to service to my country, the simplest reasons I can honestly give for joining, I might say I did this for adventure, to curb my wanderlust, to find something outside of myself, bigger than myself, to escape. Now I hate what I have become: a joke, the most hated man in my platoon. And what did I do? What have I become?

It's now nearing the end of my shift and the steady parade of tiny red lens flashlights and headlamps bobbing across the outpost would be comical were it not so utterly depressing. An army of chronic masturbators, all of them, proud and uncaring. I know they're not headed to the latrines to piss because they would never actually get out of their cot to relieve themselves, opting instead to pee into a water bottle kept stowed under their cot. I, on the other hand, stop drinking water after 1800 and make sure I use the latrine before I get to my cot because I refuse to pee in a bottle and the ruckus I would cause to get across to the front door would cost me dearly the next day in the form of push-ups or low crawling. But getting up to wack off into a steel bucket in the middle of the night is somehow okay? I made this mistake once and learned my lesson, both in discovering that at night the shit buckets are used as a masturbatorium and in the price I paid the next day when my team leader made me low crawl for thirty minutes as punishment for waking him up. It's not my fault I'm on the far end of the room.

So now, after my recitation, once the initial laughter subsided, my team leader wanted to know what the poem means. I'm not so arrogant to pretend to know myself. But I know what the poem means to me—the sense of physical awe carried in the lines that shakes me to my core—and I carry in my heart the idea that someone out there tonight cared, if even for a little bit, about what I was doing. That someone, anyone of the guys left there watching this sad display, might someday take an interest in something other than their alcohol, drugs, guns, porn, sports, and comic book movies. I can only dream.

In my response I wanted to sound intelligent to my team leader but not too intelligent, like I cared about the material but not to the point of obsession. I had to present this as just a piece of entertainment no different than their movies, just a thing I do. But this was a tall order. I was fighting an enemy of entrenched stupidity. The idea that an interest in anything other than guns and vaginas means you must love dudes. But here I was, digging my own grave. I gave my team leader some meaningless answer about how poetry means different things to different people, and I really wasn't concerned with the meaning, but rather my first concern was how the words were aligned and looked on the page, how the rhythms of each line affected me internally. I told them that poetry is not a riddle to be deciphered or solved. I told him I enjoyed the words first, the way they're ordered, like reading a map and first getting a general sense of the terrain, and that gives me an idea of how the poem will work itself out for me. Once we work past that—and I pretended to be ignorant of this poem's structure—if we really want to get down to the nuts and bolts of this one, it means nothing is real, everything we pursue will ultimately be a disappointment. I then reminded them that I'd only recited a small portion of the poem, the last eight lines of a 720-line long poem. I told them this, and this is where I hoped to hit home with some of them, that we have to figure out a way to live in the disappointment that is all human entanglements, and in some way it might be no use having big ideas and sentiments couched in tangible realities because true adventure, true love, only comes from the infinite array of life we find when we accept that we are alone. I told them that, believe it or not, I loved adventure and romanticism and all the other things that should make a soldier a soldier, the pursuit of the indefinable *it* factor—and when I said this I made a fist and shook it—that makes us who we are as warriors . . . the unknown always within reach but never attainable.

I thought I nailed it. My presentation was short and sweet and I held the room without sounding like I thought I was smarter than everybody else. I delivered my oration in a way that said I know its dumb but whatever. My team leader's reply? "Cool. Well, I like big titties," and the room erupted with laughter. The response actually could have been much worse, and I was glad he ended the whole ordeal with a joke. But I delivered my recitation and analysis with confidence and I believe I won a few people over. I think everyone was in a good mood tonight and that helped my case. I thought I'd make my escape right then and head back to my hut, but my team leader said, "Alright, Shakespeare, you're on cleaning detail," and had me report to the mess tent for work. I was impressed he could name even one writer.

I feel like I personally know Private Alastor. Not as a friend, necessarily, calling another man a friend has always felt strange to me, but a compatriot? Sure. Fellow sojourner? Yes. I fall far short of feeling sorry for him, but I do feel shame. For what, though, remains unclear. Many of Alastor's thoughts are my thoughts. Especially when I was a private. But once I wriggled my way up out of the mire, this world was left behind, a forgotten nightmare. But I remember hating that I couldn't have a conversation with anyone else about books we did not understand. I hated the lifestyle these guys lead, my peers, my countrymen, men I was prepared to give my life for should circumstances require. When I first ventured into town in my first army posting, just a young kid who had hardly ever been away from home,

I wondered why the town was filled with strip clubs and pawn shops and massage parlors that, I soon learned, offered so much more than a massage. All this within walking distance of my barracks. You will pay out your ass for a cab if you want to get to a bookstore or library or, heaven forbid, a museum. But you adapt, you put all that aside and try to internalize what it is that makes you a soldier. I move on and flip ahead:

> March 15th. I don't know how to write about what happened today. I have to find a way out. We walked about an hour to a village, the largest village in our area. We've never really had any problems here, and I like the kids here because there are a lot of them and they seem really happy when we show up. I did the usual today, pulled security. But today I was with my team leader and our team's grenadier. We were all pretty laid back for most of the day. The platoon leader held his own little meeting with some of the locals and we were really close to it and got to hear some of the back-and-forth between the lieutenant and the village elders through the interpreter. It was a really good day, and I felt like I was part of the whole ordeal as opposed to the patrols over the last few months where we endlessly walked in the mountains and didn't see anyone for days or we drove around with no action except for the rockets that get fired at us when we're home at Chemera.
>
> Things have been improving for me. Even my team leader told me I had been doing a good job and to keep up the good work. He says I'm a pretty good automatic rifleman and thinks I'll make specialist soon and wants me to start studying for things like Soldier of the Month and stuff like that. It was a beautiful day, in my spirit and in the world. But after today I'm not sure I can abide this situation any longer.
>
> I can't do anything but just say it: thirty minutes before we were scheduled to link up with the rest of the platoon, and just as we started to gather up our belongings, my team leader pissed in a water well. He stood up next to the well and peed into it, laughing. The other guy with us told him it was fucked up but he didn't care. I still can't believe it as I write it down. Why was this dude here? What did he think war was? He was respected. And truth be told, as much as I hate him for giving me such a hard time, he knew his job. He had mellowed a little bit, even, and has actually been giving me good instructions before we head out for patrols. Now he pisses in a well? What was the point? How could I live with this on my conscience? I can't snitch. Is that loyalty? And where does my loyalty lie? With my team?

Platoon? Mission? My country? I don't even know why we're here anymore.

It didn't stop there; it never does. Some of the same kids I had given most of my MRE to earlier in the day rounded the corner and saw him pissing. And there were several older kids with them as well, teenagers. When he saw that they had seen him pissing in the well he ran after them. The teenagers were long gone but he managed to catch one of the smaller kids, he couldn't have been more than seven or eight, and he slapped him twice across the face and then punched him in the gut. I saw this. I witnessed this act with my eyes. A soldier in my army pissing in a well and then beating a kid. And my friend and I just stood there.

When the team leader came back we asked him what in the fuck he was doing. All respect for rank and structure was out the window. The team leader said he knew he had sort of fucked up by being seen so he couldn't let the kids go; they'd tell the elders and then we'd have a shit storm on our hands. But he couldn't catch them all, and he wasn't sure what he would do anyway if he caught one. But when he did catch one of the small kids, he thought if he punched him a few times or left a red mark on his face, the elders might think the teenagers had beat the kid up and were now cooking up a story about the foreign soldiers to try and hide it. It was worth a shot, he said. Maybe the teenagers were already well-known fuckups. My team leader said all this and then told us to keep our mouths shut. That we were both weirdos in the platoon and no one would believe us anyway. Then he added, "Especially you, Alastor."

Yes, especially me.

I am disrupted deep within my soul. And I feel for Alastor. I could now pinpoint the exact moment this soldier—a deserter and traitor to our nation—reached his breaking point. He could no longer live as his books had taught him to live, as he strived to live. Alastor was now incapable of doing exactly what the ancients have instructed. He had not yet built his wall of indifference. He had not yet created two worlds within himself, one at war and one pretending to not be at war.

I wonder why the investigator is taking so long. How will he read these entries? What will his reaction be? Has the investigator built any sort of wall inside of himself? The last entry I read, written the week before he walked to the enemy:

April 11: My soul is at peace. I am ready. To do my duty. To
honor my true nature. To love my country. To do the unthinkable. The next chance I get.

I hear the first sergeant and the major coming down the narrow hallway towards the aid station, and I quickly shut the book and slide it behind
my back under my shirt, securing the book by my belt, the words *to do the
unthinkable* echoing in my head as the big sliding door is pushed open and
the duo step inside the aid station. I feign annoyance as I stare down at
Alastor's belongings, awaiting the full entrance of the major so that I can
say, on cue:

"What a piece of shit."

"Come on, Captain, we don't know that for sure until the investigation
is complete."

And we all laugh.

19.

Alastor's journal is a cry for help from someone who does not understand what is happening around him, a futile writing exercise in which he attempts to justify his own thoughts and reconcile the places and events in which he now finds himself with his beliefs. I undertook a writing exercise myself as an adolescent, a writing exercise in which I wrote in the first person about events that had already taken place in the form of a series of journal entries. This seemed to me, at the time, the most logical way to write a novel and the easiest way in which to tell the story I had in mind. This exercise, of course, predates any of my own journal keeping, sporadic as it has been.

I was in sixth grade when I began to write this story on a white legal pad in the back of my tri-fold notebook. The style I chose for my novel, besides being a first-person account of past events as they unfolded for the narrator, was what is known as a choose-your-own-adventure novel. The specifics of the novel are vague, though I do recall the primary character and the exact mission on which he had embarked. The story could only be categorized as a science fiction novel, as the action took place outside our own galaxy. This also seemed like the easiest way in which to manipulate time and space in a book designed to force the reader to hop from place to place within the book and to best keep the active reader engaged with a series of decisions they would make based on the subconscious feelings one gets when at the beginning of a book, the middle, or near the end. This feeling of time and decision-making in the book needed to be a tangible reality so as to best guide the reader along based on how the pages in their hand felt. I did not then, nor do I now, possess an affinity for science fiction. I was only fascinated by the possibilities of a story in which concepts of time and place could be so easily manipulated.

What came out in my writing exercise then was a story less about a space adventure and more about jumping back and forth in a notebook based on what I thought the reader would think were their own decision-making processes but were actually decisions made based on the subconscious effects of where they thought they were in the text. I fretted over how the book was formed and counted the pages to exactly match where I wanted each choice to take a reader.

This fascination with the feel of the book in the reader's hand soon gave way to what I discovered was my true motivation: that my teacher see me engaged in this lone activity and then view me as someone who needed to find patterns and stability within the pages of a legal pad in the back of a tripartite folder. Whenever we were provided free time to read library books, I took out my tri-fold notebook and began to work on my choose-your-own-adventure science fiction fantasy novel until eventually the teacher noticed my work and took an interest in me as a budding writer. Though I wish she had taken an interest in me as a budding planner.

I most often went about my writing during free time in the class, as I never remember writing anywhere but in that classroom, in one specific seat, a seat which was chosen for me on the first day. The seat was chosen for me because that is how these things are done in a room full of twelve-year-olds. You dream of the day when, in future classrooms, you will have the freedom to saunter into the classroom and sit wherever you like but, when that day arrives, everyone sits in the same place they sat on day one lest you upset the entire order of things and cause a ripple effect of changed seats and upended choices that were each individually and freely made on the first day and will from here on out define your understanding of the spaces within the universe that is this classroom.

Besides free time, this teacher who took an interest in me as an aspiring writer also spent considerable class time having students read aloud from chapters in a textbook. We went up and down the rows, with each student in turn reading a paragraph with, I am quite certain, no comprehension or retention of what was just read. I for one certainly never paid attention to what was being said by my classmates. Instead, I counted out paragraphs so that I might review the paragraph I would be assigned in hopes it was a long one and I could show off my reading and oratory skills. Having done this, and sufficiently secure in my abilities to accomplish the task at hand, I still did not go back and listen to what was being read by my classmates, but rather I counted out each potential paragraph assignment so as to ascertain whether or not any of the slower readers in the class were to be assigned a difficult passage. I hoped that they were given short, easy-to-read paragraphs, as it pained me to listen to them struggle over even the simplest of texts. It did not occur to me until many years later that the slow readers might have very well been doing the same thing as me in hopes that they would not be burdened with a long, difficult passage to read and thus expose themselves once again as a slow reader. I feel bad for not making this realization until well into adulthood.

But once this teacher noticed my writing exercise and I was satisfied that she recognized and appreciated my reading abilities, I stopped my writing exercise altogether and gave up the very idea of writing a choose-your-own-adventure novel so that now, whenever I pick up a notebook to once again begin my sporadic journaling, I feel as if I am again in this teachers' classroom, and I lose the ability to recognize whether I am the age I was in sixth grade, the age I am now when the events are taking place, or the age I will be somewhere far down the line in the future. Events no longer exist on a linear timeline, but rather exist at all moments across the course of human history.

Such is the feeling of planning a second mission into Gaumela. We did what we were supposed to do the first time and then some. We poked around in a potential hornet's nest and got ourselves into a thrilling little skirmish. Mission success. That first mission to Gaumela now becomes all moments for us, an expansion of time, the feel of the event overlaying itself over this entire combat tour. With or without Alastor.

Our second mission to the border may be judged differently, if history makes any assessment of the actions of a single infantry company in a war now dwarfed by whatever war in an unknown foreign land looms on the horizon. The order to go back into Gaumela a second time came as a surprise. The search for Alastor does not seem to be going well, as everyone across the country has dropped their primary mission and is focused on finding this lone soldier, to no avail. We all know that he is no longer in this country. Further, the rumor that he walked away, that he is in fact a deserter, is now firmly established throughout every echelon of command—from the private pumping fuel at a sprawling airbase to the drone pilot plying his trade in a bunker somewhere in our home country, and all the way back around to the general in a dark, map-filled room at our nation's military headquarters—everyone knows Alastor left of his own volition. And yet the search goes on.

And while I agree with this sentiment in its philosophic logic, in application it is a recipe for disaster. For I know that something stirs in Gaumela. Our first operation there, with a decisive engagement and the declaration of imminent threat, should have sent up red flags to Higher that something smells in this border village and the more we go poking around without full clearance to lock down and clear the village the more we invite trouble. I cannot imagine the insurgents who have sought safe haven in and around this border village believed we would stop short of clearing the entire village. What invading force would stop short of clearing the land they wish to occupy of all its inhabitants, of all its previous thoughts and deeds and ways and patterns of life? The enemy knows this is madness, as do I. If you are mad enough to show your power then remove that power without hooking your barb into the lands from which you have decided to exact your revenge, then it is quite possible your nation deserves whatever fate hands you.

I do not shy away from trouble nor from the idea of showing up to my piece of the fight with overwhelming force. With the same basic plan in place, the element of surprise, and a liberal interpretation of the need to declare *imminent threat* on the border, my men and I can continue to stir the pot and make the enemy show his cards. Yet I cannot help but think, even though I love my men and the capabilities of our nation's military, and even though I have full confidence in my own abilities as a tactical leader, that a more surgical operation should take place with a unit designed for such operations, a small unit trained for precise operations, not a unit trained to wreak havoc on a situation, to *spray and pray*, to saturate and *disrupt* and kill, in a general sense.

"You doing the same thing you did last time, sir?" The XO asks as he sits at his desk in the corner and shuffles papers—hand receipts, logistical requests, Class I reports—in an unorganized pile of chaos that he thinks if he stacks enough times will magically organize themselves into self-selecting piles. I know why he is asking. Or rather, I know why he has framed the question like this.

"You want to go this time, XO?"

"I'm good, sir. I mean, I will, if you need me to. But I think I'm needed here instead."

Fair enough. I know this kid, and I know his deployment history. He got three months' time on the tail end of a deployment when he was a fresh second lieutenant and saw little, if any, combat. He has the requisite badges now required of an infantry officer, badges that will take him as far as he wants to go in his career. Which does not seem very far. Is he just lazy or is he looking out for his own safety? Indifferent perhaps?

"Yeah, I need you here to man the radios and relay info for me."

"That's what I do best, sir. But why *are* we going back? Just out of curiosity."

"Do we need a reason?"

"I don't suppose."

"If you really want to know, I guess we're going back because we're here. And we've been given orders."

"Sounds good to me."

This is a true statement. So I have come to believe. I have a job to do and intend to do it within the limitations set forth by my leaders and by our nation's foreign policy directives, regardless of circumstances and regardless of the current situation. And it is also true that the best place for this young officer, for both the company and the mission, is to remain here at Chemera. Regardless of his past experience or his desires, the team needs him to remain on site, not go on mission. And he seems comfortable with this. Which irks me. He should be raring to get out the gate. I should have to rein him in and prevent him from going out on missions. Instead, he sits at his desk, dutifully sends his reports higher, and receives and distributes logistical supplies when they come in via helicopter, all things a good company executive officer does. There is no reason for me to question his motivation or his drive. He has a role, a role that he knows and is comfortable with.

Yet I want him to do more war fighting and I do not know why. I did my time as an XO and was never comfortable in the position, watching patrols go out while I sat by and organized spreadsheets of meals and ammunition, beans and bullets. But just like the feelings I have regarding the behavior of my own executive officer, I do not know if the reluctance to give my all to the performance of my duties during my time as an XO was a result of laziness, fear of failure, or indifference. Was I simply secure in the knowledge that my role no longer called for me to be out with my fellow infantrymen every time they went on a mission, and so I was able to exhibit a certain level of bravado knowing I was to stay behind and distribute supplies? Make no mistake, I went on many combat missions as an XO, mostly to serve as a liaison between my company commander and resupply efforts for extended patrols. But on more than one occasion I was tasked with pushing resupply out to the men from the relative safety of a larger base. And I loathed these taskings. Or at least I pretended to.

I know that deep down inside the possibility exists that my own exhibitions of bravery were simply efforts to hide my fear, that the eternal life found in a true soldier is not found in me. I am continuously haunted in particular by one mission as an XO in which, during a long vehicular convoy before the advent of the large iron-clad behemoths we skulk around the battlefield in now, and back when we conducted convoys in more traditional up-armored all-terrain vehicles, I chose on one resupply mission to sit in the back seat. And my fear is that I chose to ride in the back seat out of a subconscious fear that the back seat was safer for me as a leader should we become engaged in a firefight or come across an underground bomb or makeshift mine designed to destroy the vehicle and its human contents. Several other leaders—though still a tiny minority of the overall convoy—more experienced than me at the time, particularly in mounted warfare, had opted to position themselves in the backseat under the argument that there was more room to do map checks, talk on the radio, and utilize and track the myriad global positioning system trackers and various accoutrement that have become standard in most motorized patrols. I took them at their word. At least I pretended to. I cannot know at the time whether or not my decision was based in fear or if I had rationalized this position in the backseat, counter to everything I had been taught as a leader, as the better position from which I could best lead and support my element. There is in fact more room in the back to maintain operational checklists, send radio reports, check maps, et cetera, et cetera. But this is not the point. The point is whether or not I chose to position myself in the back seat because I felt it was a safer place for me, the leader. At the time, I gave no thought to the matter. At least that is what I tell myself. But once the issue crept into my brain, the question grew and grew until now, many years later, I have no doubts that my entire decision was based in a subconscious fear for which I have endeavored to make up for every day of my life since. For fear has no place in things eternal. It is this belief I carry with me into the second mission to the border village of Gaumela.

This second plan needs to be as bold, audacious, and fearless, as the first. Different, but only slightly. We caught the enemy completely off guard, as I suspect he has grown used to an opponent who generally stays in a combat outpost and shuffles out for the occasional patrol. It has been many years since a conventional company executed a coordinated deliberate attack on a target. And frankly, at this point, we are alone, left to fend for ourselves by a distracted hierarchy on a distracting mission: the solo infantry company venturing into the borderlands to pick a fight. I do not need to justify my actions to anyone. Let's get this job done the way it should have been done countless years ago, a re-awakening of the soldier's spirit on the loop of eternal combat so that we may move on as we see fit, on to the next objective, on to the next fight.

Based on feedback from leaders on the ground during the first skirmish in Gaumela, we are adjusting positions only slightly, making a few shifts here and there only to get a better vantage point from which to engage the enemy. We want all of them this time. And we want him to concentrate his fire on where he thinks we were last time.

Certainly the enemy was shaken during our first fight on the hill. Shaken to the point of possibly elevating his own tactics for the future. But our plan was solid and will remain so. If it isn't broken, there is no reason to fix it. The only thing we can do is become more bold, confident, and strong in our occupation of this slice of the AO. And this need for audacity is where my interpreter comes in.

All the tools at my disposal for waging war are the same and all are perfectly sane and legitimate. My motives, however, and the object of my work is where I enjoy a degree of leniency in my sanity. The application of my tools is only limited by my imagination. And so it is that I have called upon my interpreter to carry a bullhorn into battle and make a series of announcement from our mountain hide site to both the villagers of Gaurela and to the enemy who chooses to hide behind an international border no one seems to care about except our nation and our nation's army. This is the bold, audacious action that will take the battle to the next operational level and let the enemy know that we mean business, that whatever they are hiding nearby, whatever methods they are using to disguise their actions in and around my company's area of operations, will be short-lived.

The rest of the mission remains the same. I sleep peaceably the night before this mission, reading my book about whaling, and rocked to sleep in this vast sea of unconquered time and space.

20.

0300. I GIVE MY rousing speech at the front gate before our movement into the dark of night, across the desert floor and into the borderlands that make up our current fight. The movement to our various release points proves much more troublesome this time—a misdirection, a piece of bad communication, a neglected component of the execution checklist missed—than in our first foray into the mountains. During a long halt the first sergeant makes his way to the front of the formation to find me in the pitch black.

"These feel like some bad omens, sir. The men aren't ready, and it's pissing me off."

"Ah, we'll be alright, First Sergeant. We all know what's coming and we should face it head on. Laugh a bit too, eh? We're about to get after it. Stick it to 'em, ya know? The men are just excited and letting the little things get in the way."

He was not buying it, but I do not have time for his pessimism. I announce into the dark silence, "What are we waiting for? The second coming? Let's get moving."

The titters and under-the-breath *hooahs* delivered with the perfect mix of false motivation and sarcasm let me know the men are as ready as they will ever be. We are five hundred meters from the release point, the spot where each individual element will split off into its own area of operations.

0430. The rocky terrain beneath my feet reaches out and grabs my ankles with each step, a hazard in the approach march unnoticed in the excitement of the first operation to Gaumela and I suddenly come to the realization that the trek is much harder than I initially thought. After only one trip here my body has already developed a reluctance to climb these hills again. My nature already knows what is in store and wants no part of it. I must fight my nature in order to keep moving to my objective, the object of my obsession.

The acknowledgment of my physical self to the difficulties ahead comes quicker than usual. But trauma repeated through time and repetition builds the inertia needed to do my job. This recognition comes sooner than it should, and I push back against the idea that this is another sign of a potentially bad outing, a situation in which you may likely already know the outcome, or you may not, given our country's propensity for overlooking the details of combat in exchange for a simplified wins-versus-losses, great-battles narrative. My concern on this jagged hillside in which my interpreter also seems to struggle with just the added encumbrance of a bullhorn is that my psyche has figured out a way in which to recognize hardship and difficulties and thus signals mistakes and foibles much sooner than has been typical in my life.

Such is my fear now. That my physical nature has accelerated the process so that I am being sent information in the present that tells me I am not up to the standards required for proper mission accomplishment. What have typically been revelations many years after the event have now suddenly accelerated to reveal themselves right now, on the side of this mountain, in the dark, with a company of paratroopers trusting in my leadership. On the side of a mountain before going to start a fight on a border between two countries, one at war with an insurgency and one pretending to not be supportive of that insurgency, is not the time for a revelatory experience in which you realize all the mistakes you have made in your life but never realized until now that they were actual mistakes. In the distance, a rock tumbles down the side of the hill, and I wonder how an untied canteen may be linked to this sound.

I have selected a different point man for my element on this mission, and I immediately regret the decision. He is lost and is pinpointing his location through justifications grounded in laziness. The rest of us can feel his insecurity and anxieties as he mentally turns tiny hilltops that should take minimal effort into major terrain features. Another stop for a map check and word is sent back that *we're here*.

We are where? He has no idea. We are barely halfway to where we need to be. Frustrated, I move to the front of the formation, tripping over two of my men sprawled out on their backs in a rucksack flop.

"Sit up, Airborne," and I get no response.

My radioman is right on my heels and, as always, is itching for a fight, his motivation and energy palpable, his own frustration with the incompetence of the point man visible in the dark morning. But I know as we move the twenty meters from the middle of the formation through the scattering of the nine-man element that he is patting his peers on the helmet or giving them a slap on their legs as if to say *he's just in one of his moods, it's okay.*

I do not stop when I reach the point man and make the immediate turn required to get us back on azimuth and up to the crest of the next hill looming directly in front us. The artillery lieutenant and the interpreter are struggling to catch up, and I know I just made a mess of the whole movement order. I should stop and get a head count, make sure the machine gun team in the rear knows what is happening and that the sudden gap in the movement has not disoriented them, but I do not. They will figure it out.

"Get an update from the other elements, little camper," I whisper-yell back to my radioman.

"You breathing hard, sir?"

"What? Go fuck yourself."

I take the opportunity to motivate my radioman, and myself, as we try to salvage what is quickly becoming a train wreck of an operation.

"What's wrong with these guys this morning? The mission! The mission! We've all been here before. By God, am I the only one that cares anymore?"

"This is all true, sir. They're being sad clowns," my radioman says.

"Ha. Well let's you and I do this thing, then, if they don't want to play."

"Always, sir."

He calls the other positions and the responses are immediate. I know then and there that no one has a firm grasp on their position. But I push on, secure in the knowledge that we have been here before. We did this exact operation just a week prior. We have done this exact mission since time immemorial. A feint, a decoy, an ambush, it has all been done before and it will all be done again and again. Just get to a place. And wait.

21.

THE FIRST RAYS OF the sun come barreling over the mountains and I confirm that none of us are where we should be. We are all kinds of screwed up, and we know it, despite the clear, quiet, and illuminating morning. It's too late to turn back now. There is too much at stake. My radioman gets refined grids to everyone's position, and when I scan across the valley at the other position silhouetting itself in the morning light it becomes clear that each element is not where they have reported themselves to be. They have checked the box and slid into the first available spot. They have gone through the motions. A fine line exists between indifference and confidence, and it becomes difficult to pinpoint whether the men just no longer give a shit or whether they felt so good after the last skirmish that they are just overeager for a new spray-and-pray opportunity and let the finer details of the operation slip away in their execution.

Time for a cigarette. My crew passes around two smokes, dissipating the smoke with a wave of the hand as if these maneuvers would never give away our position in mountains that are only ever occupied by goats and invading armies. My element and I are short about a hundred meters from where we need to be, having stopped in a small hillside depression during a halt and letting fatigue convince me that this spot was good enough. And it might very well be good enough. But just.

The white sun has risen much too high now for us to move. There is a boulder three of us can safely take cover behind, but we are shoulder to shoulder; the other six in our party stay low in the depression on the back side of the hill but still just ten meters from me, my radioman, the interpreter, and the big rock. I give instructions that no one is to even peek over the hill, as it is too easy to spot even the smallest item out of order on a hillside you have stared at your entire life. We will do all our reconnaissance from behind this boulder and the few scattered smaller rocks nearby in an attempt to blend with the jagged horizon provided by this exposed outcropping.

The men in the other two positions are easily identified from this vantage point. They are moving about freely and a lone head will pop up now and again giving up their position. Just as no career soldier should be provided two distinct wars to fight, I now know no soldier should be asked to repeat a mission, certainly not this soon after the first. The effects of the first skirmish will linger, rendering the second skirmish an afterthought, impossible to rise to the occasion on the same piece of terrain a mere week or two later. By the same token, the lifetime soldier cannot overcome the effects of his generation's war and will apply all the lessons learned from his campaign onto a new war for which new lessons must be learned by a new generation, a generation new to the soldier's loop. For our purposes here on this mountain we should have considered the job complete the first time and either moved on to another mission in the search for Alastor or hunkered down just outside Jacuz, out of range of small arms, snooped around for a few hours pretending to patrol, then moved back in to Chemera and to a hot dinner.

Our trucks begin to rumble in the distance just as a child, not more than seven or eight years old, saunters up and around the backside of the hill and approaches our position from the rear. A brave little soul living his one life on this small mountaintop. You may believe what you want. But those of us in this mountain hide site will not debate what this boy is doing. There will be no ethical decision-making process, no wringing of hands, no fretting over his purpose. He is not discussed, spoken of, nor spoken to. He is ignored as he stares at us from a safe distance until the interpreter looks at me long and hard, turns away, and says something to the boy in his language. He then scampers back down the mountain side.

My artillery lieutenant looks at me with incredulity and I know what everyone is thinking.

"Ya'll watch too many movies. He's a kid looking for his goats. Nothing more," and I go back to scanning the border, waiting for the first signs of life to come bounding over the crest and into my waiting and eager sights.

The trucks arrive in backward order from what I briefed, a decision apparently made on the fly when a water can fell off the lead truck and the rest played a sort of leap frog while they retrieved their cargo. It's not a big deal but indicative of the day's events on the whole, and I still do not view any of these events as omens necessarily but rather as normal parts of an infantry mission. What matters is the end state. What matters is that the first insurgent comes bounding over the hill in full view, ready to be put down.

The trucks settle in and I order my interpreter to commence his announcements over the bullhorn, to make that bullhorn echo throughout the valley. I feed him the lines to which he translates, the words of his language sounding even sharper, more haunting than the lines I feed him:

"We know you are hiding behind this border because you will not fight us like men. You are cowards afraid to face us. Keep launching rockets at our base if you want. But we are here now, so come fight."

I grab the radio hand mic and ask my other positions if they can hear us, if these announcements are crossing over to their positions.

"Loud and clear."

"That sounds awesome, sir."

"That's some creepy shit, sir."

I feel good in the moment. Present. Waiting on an earth with no borders.

And there he is now, just the tiniest of silhouettes on the horizon. The first enemy to show himself this day. This one is bold and fearless in all his fervent glory, zigzagging down the hill back and forth, his man-dress and shawl flowing in the breeze. He stops at a large rock and looks at the trucks. We all see him, each and every one of us. We each imagine putting him out of his misery, wondering who will get to take the shot that ends his life. The position just to the right of ours and slightly below gets on the radio and is the first to ask permission to put him down.

"Do you got him?"

"Oh, I got him."

"Stand by One-seven, let me get *imminent threat* cleared through Battalion."

And as my radioman raises Chemera on the net to act as relay to Battalion, the barrage begins. The *ping* and *zing* of machine gun fire whizzes by my head, near misses all, and I cannot get low enough to the ground nor tell from which direction the firing is coming. When you have done this long enough it becomes easy to tell if rounds being fired at you are presenting a real danger or if it is poorly-aimed shots from a distance. But I do not know right now. I have lost my ability to tell the differences with these rounds whizzing by my head. Each flurry snaps off crisp and sure in the clear air and I remember that my mountain fights are few and far between. Most of my combat has taken place in the villages, around mud walls, into darkened breaches, down alleyways and across orchards, in fields of freshly grown crops and in hastily constructed rooftop fortresses. The angles here are different. I stay low between my radioman and my interpreter, all three of us with heads bowed in silent prayer.

The firing stops and I see my artillery lieutenant still in the depression roll onto his side, conferring with his NCO, and the two commence their own work of bringing in mortar fire. I pick my head up in search of our lone enemy frolicking across the mountainside a few moments earlier, now nowhere to be found. My radioman is sending a report up to Chemera and I tell him to keep it real simple as we let this thing develop. I am not entirely sure what just happened, and I need to get an idea from the other positions what just took place.

"I got no good ID."

"Sounds like they're in a hide site, too."

"I lost him, sir. Dude just vanished from the hillside as soon as the shooting started."

"Did we just get flanked, sir?"

"We're good down in the trucks. No effects."

No one knows anything. All is quiet. I tell my interpreter to get back on the bullhorn and let them have it. This time, I do not feed him lines, I just let him go and he sounds even harsher, more evil than before.

Five minutes pass and now two insurgents come over the hillside bounding and bouncing along the spine of the ridgeline just at my two-o'clock but out of a comfortable range.

"I can get him again, sir. I got this one," comes the chatter from the position below us.

"Kill him, One-seven."

A long seven seconds pass before we hear the crack and then witness the lead insurgent slump and somersault down the side of the hill before crumbling to a stop on the slope. He scrambles back up, taking cover behind a small boulder, when the machine guns open up again. Both sides, back and forth, firing into nothing. My radioman begins to make a radio transmission back to Chemera that we are again in contact when he jerks toward me in one single motion. He lets out what sounds like a laugh, "Ha . . . Ha," and slams his head into the rocky dirt.

"What's the matter, Junior? Getting a little too close for comfort?"

I wish I could tell you more . . . but I will not. You either already know his name or you do not. He is every soldier you have ever met, every soldier you have ever read about, every soldier you have ever sent into battle, every soldier you know exists somewhere in a world you have never seen in a distant galaxy, *choosing his own adventure.* He is anonymous and that distant cousin of yours. Anonymous and the child of your coworker. Anonymous and your own son or daughter. Anonymous and the name on a pedestal in your hometown at the roadside park no one goes to. Anonymous and never known. Anonymous and never forgotten. His nation's blood left on a boulder near a border between two countries, one at war with an insurgency and one pretending to not be supporting that insurgency.

Dear reader, I do not believe that you would send us to do what we do without some expectation of death. But the fear of death does not live in us, nor is death ours to give. This is how a soldier understands the eternal. His true life is found in death. For without the soldier's courage to die a physical death, he knows there is no life in him. So you may settle in with your expectations . . . and wait.

I grab my radioman's fist, still clenching the hand mic, open up his hand, and massage what warmth remains in his slender fingers. His eyes were blank the moment he cried out: *Ha . . . Ha*. This is the only action I can take to move him from one world to another, to release him from his sacred duty.

The mountaintop goes silent. Holy once more. Releasing his fingers, I touch his cheek with the back of my fingers. He hasn't shaved in two days. Neither have I.

Grabbing the hand mic I give the order to withdraw and then bandage my radioman's mortal wound the best I can and cover his rugged, stoic, now-lifeless face for the trip home. We begin to scramble down the side of the mountain, not each element in its turn via a planned withdrawal. No. Not that. We crawl and roll and drag our defeated bodies back down the rocky hillside. I wish it were not so. But our nation, a nation I love and cherish with all my heart, does not leave a fallen comrade. He cannot stay here, though I know his wishes were the same as mine: to remain in the place where he is taken off the loop. But this is not our policy. And we have a job to do.

The enemy has chosen not to close the distance, though they could. And they still might while we are so *disrupted*. But when you are evacuating a fellow soldier off the field of battle, you give no thought to security measures or to the possibility you are being flanked or to what happened five minutes prior or to what will happen in the future. You only hope the enemy's pride willfully stands down to your vanity and arrogance. You only know you are in a present in which you want out. A present in which time has been left behind. To think about the future is to acknowledge this time. Whatever will be will be. The enemy, that which I have come to know as my enemy, has chosen to execute a hit-and-run operation and now no longer exists, if he ever did, basking in his victory. This is the mission we conducted a week prior. But we went to the well one too many times. And we have been *disrupted*.

22.

My imaginary baseball game kept the world at bay until the world could no longer be contained, until the world forced itself onto me and I was deployed to combat in defense of our nation's foreign policy objectives, and was forced to see truth in all its unifying reality. The life created for us is a facade—names, numbers, statistics, policies, and standards—a mask to be ripped to shreds, exposing the nature of all endeavors as mere illusions: borderless, without margin, numberless, and nameless. There are no teams, no places, no homes, just meaningless events in an imaginary game created to pass the crushing movement of time.

The numbers bleed, bleed everywhere, bleed all together when the game is played on a continual loop. Only the game changes and a new set of rules must be applied to each generation so that the present feels like it is outstripping the past. But it never has. This *new game* in which the old benchmarks of success no longer apply turns the cogs in the machine. And we either try to keep up or find a way out of the game.

It should be obvious to you by now, dear reader, that the players in my game were never given names. To give them names would have been to ascribe life upon them and thus unite the worlds that had to be kept apart at all costs because we now know that once these lives come into contact with one another, the crushing weight of the truth becomes too much to bear.

And now here I am, telling you this, and thinking of my radioman whose name you do not know, whose name is with me always, even in those rare moments when I am able to sit and watch the sunset and stare off into the distant mountains and dream of my home, a home that gets closer with each breath as I wonder if he even heard my final words to him:

Getting a little too close for comfort?

I cannot help but believe that you may see things differently now. I cannot know whether what you wanted, what you required of those you send to do your bidding, is a good captain with a bad attitude or a happily lockstep bad captain. I now know what will happen both before and after you read these words. I know my actions and I know your actions. I have always known. So if I say I am writing this now or then, in the moment of my radioman's death or many years after, you will not know on which side of the margin I stand, only that I stand somewhere taking notes outside of myself, nameless and anonymous, in my mind a moody good captain who has forever failed his men and himself. But the universe takes what the universe desires and I am in no position to argue with the natural order of things.

In this moment, as you read this, I am telling of events in the present, such as they are in the my past, such as they ever will be. In this moment a soldier is dead in the search for Alastor. Others have died as well. The body count grows in the search for a man who deserted our country. Depending on where you stand in relation to the borders that have been constructed for us, you may play a shell game in which additional soldiers did not die looking for Alastor, they died as part of normal patrol cycles or the natural rhythms of war or because fate deemed it so. This is what you will believe. Then so be it.

The necessary rituals of seeing our soldier, my radioman, returned to our home nation and to his final resting place have been conducted. The rest of the company remains in Chemera. The battalion staff has repositioned themselves back at Palermo and has turned Jacuz back over to the people to live as they have lived for hundreds of years prior to our arrival. My men and I have not been out on patrol since the second battle of Gaumela.

I am to be visited once again by the battalion commander and, I know what is about to happen. We will have a long discussion about the way ahead, about the next steps to be taken, and likely about my future with the organization. This is an inevitable conversation that must be had. I do not look forward to it.

It would have been easier for me as an officer if I never put together a detailed and complex plan and instead created broad brush strokes. Simple orders cannot be parsed apart for blame. People only grade that which you provide them to evaluate. But a detailed order will be judged for every fault that can be found, faults that would not have even been evaluated were the plan to simply patrol from point A to point B. But because I put a hard line on the paper, created a detailed system of movements, these actions will each be judged on their individual merits. In this case, a soldier was not killed because of war's nebulosity. A soldier was killed because of one officer's hubris, a failure to account for enemy evolution, perhaps a misguided trust in a local child on a hillside, and possibly even an interpreter. The truth, though, is that a detailed plan takes tragedy out of the hands of the fates and places it squarely on the officer's shoulders. This forms the weight of command, as it should. Pinpoint directives elicit detailed post-action analysis. Broad brushstrokes can be written off as collateral damage in the conduct of a dangerous business.

I get the speech on the first night of the battalion commander's visit after a day of him talking to *the boys*, of getting a feel for the level of morale in the unit and walking in that peculiar modern officer way of pretending you are not an officer and are still somehow relatable to the everyday common foot soldier.

I have retreated to my big barn to watch the sunset and to wait. This is where he finds me. He pulls up an MRE box and acts nonplussed by the whole situation. I offer him a cigarette which he declines.

"Let me just get right to it, Captain. You're a good officer and a good company commander. But you're being replaced."

I light my cigarette and take the first long drag that pulls the distant mountains in closer. Prolonged eye contact with my boss eludes me, but I am able to manage a glance in his direction before turning my gaze back to my home tucked neatly away in a distant valley. I sense he is nervous.

"How long have you been in?"

"I hit eighteen next month, sir."

"Well, you'll be okay, then. We're not calling this a relief-for-cause necessarily, but you *are* being replaced before your command time is complete, and your OER will reflect this."

A part of me feels good, absolved of the responsibility to manage this ridiculous outpost in a ridiculous location, in a ridiculous situation, in a ridiculous war. But my career, such as it is, is done. I will hang on for another two or three years, find a dull staff job somewhere, and retire quietly, riding off into the sunset.

"Your replacement will be here tomorrow morning. I am trusting you to be a professional and to conduct the proper inventories with him over the next week, get him properly signed for your company, and then we'll get you out of here."

"Yes, sir," I tell him while still staring into the distance, then lowering my head to stare at the ground in front of me so as to not give away the sense of relief I actually feel.

"The colonel wants you relieved-for-cause and yanked out of here right now. But I convinced him to just give you a poor rating and give you the week to do the transition. There's too much trauma and turmoil involved in having a bad changeover and potential supply issues at this point."

"Yes, sir," I repeat into the dirt in front of me.

"When your replacement gets here tomorrow morning he'll get off the bird and I'll get on and head back to Palermo until I come back for the change of command. You spend the week showing him the ropes. I want a full left-seat, right-seat ride. Understood?"

"Yes, sir," and I pick my head back up and look towards the mountains once again.

"You took chances and risks that are not actions of a good officer. And you created a command climate in which you had a soldier desert in the middle of a firefight. These actions are indefensible. Regardless of what I think or what you think or anyone else thinks of your abilities. It's time you were taken out of command. We'll finish all the admin counseling and paperwork when we get back. Are we clear here?"

"Yes, sir," I say for the last time as we stand together, and I finally look him in the eye, once again reminded that I have a soldier who just made the ultimate sacrifice for his country and one who deserted his country and I am straddling a border even now because I am responsible for both losses. I am responsible for everything that does and does not happen in my company, on Chemera. And these two events happened.

You should know that I have always considered myself a lifer, a career soldier, from the day I first put on a uniform. I am a career soldier with a previously sparkling, impeccable record of success. A career soldier who felt he had found the place where he belonged. Finally. Until circumstance changed and lines of demarcation began to bleed into one another.

23.

I HAVE ALWAYS BEEN unsure as to how long I will remain in service to my country once these wars are over. But the writing is now on the wall. A single bad evaluation is enough to end an officer's career. My chances of ever seeing another promotion are zero, and I will be asked to leave the service after I am passed over, even if I wanted to stay. I get the sense the wars of my generation are winding down anyway. Our will to power has lost momentum, lost focus in a cause our great nation once found important. Part of the job, though. Such as it is.

Knowing that this will to power is fleeting, feeling the imminent end to this power, I have, over the past few years, crafted and honed what will constitute my ever-evolving retirement speech, to be given in front of a group of soldiers impelled to attend a ceremony they care nothing about, forced to listen to an old, retiring soldier ramble on about his career. The soldiers in attendance would not know me, of course. How could they? How could they know what I know? Mostly young, as soldiers must be, these patriots would likely not have seen their own combat yet. They would have no frame of reference for anything I tell them. These soldiers, who love their country as much as you and I, only see an old soldier who has been *over there* once upon a time and has returned a washed-up shell of a man, a staff officer putzing around in administrative duties, waiting to hit the wall. He can no longer feel useful to his nation's foreign policy projections. *Time to retire, old timer. Move on. Our turn.* But how does one convey the meaning behind a lifetime of soldiering?

I have only just recently finished this retirement speech, constructed over several gut-wrenching thought sessions during my last few weeks here at Chemera. In this retirement ceremony scenario, I make slow but bold, commanding strides to the podium, a last chance to shine before hanging up my spurs. I am not in my modern military dress blues, but have once again donned the uniform of a cavalry officer from our nation's frontier years, when my nation was at war with the indigenous peoples of the land we now call home. A jaunty wide-brimmed Stetson and loosely tied red scarf stand out amidst an otherwise dusty and sweaty uniform. I remove the service revolver from its holster and place the piece on the podium. No words spoken yet, just a slow, grandiose, visual survey of the audience. Pulling out my silver flask from an inside coat pocket, I take a big swig of whiskey, place the flask down next to the pistol with authority, and begin:

> Soldiers, I was given two very important pieces of advice early in my career. One: when in charge, be in charge. Two: when given an audience, say exactly what you need to say. So I ask you now to go with me on this journey and listen very carefully to what I'm about to tell you, because right now, I happen to be in charge for the last time in my career, and I intend to say exactly what I need to say.

I adopt the loud stentorian tone that is my public-speech-making custom, a custom that makes my words come out much too fast for the audience to keep up, words rolling off my tongue without me actually hearing what I am saying, as if speaking with headphones on. I continue:

> Here's what I have figured out. And it took me over twenty years to figure this out, but I'm giving you this information now in hopes that maybe one, just one of you, might understand and carry it with you in your own forays into combat, and war, and what you may well believe to be service to a nation. Here is what I now know and what I want you to know that I know:
>   I have been a fool. A blissfully ignorant fool. There is nothing wrong with this. In fact, this foolishness and ignorance is quite necessary to our existence. Let me explain. You, like me, probably think you were made to be a soldier. That this is all you have ever wanted to be. You, like me, consider yourself a well-rounded and successful product of our nation's system of governance and education. You are our nation's hope in a time of need, the humble servant prepared to give your life to the ideals the people of our nation hold dear. This belief applies to all aspects of our lives. Whether we at one time considered ourselves outdoorsmen, businessmen, mechanics, farmers, artists, athletes, or all of the above, we have voluntarily given up these endeavors in order to serve something bigger than ourselves. But yet, something is not quite right, is it? Even now you realize there are certain aspects of the career you weren't banking on. This is by design. For it requires a level of cognitive dissonance,

of this blissful ignorance of which I speak, to navigate this mighty machine we call our nation's army. For we are all guided by something outside of ourselves that accounts for where we are now, that accounts for our current lot in life, that accounts for our allegiance to a system designed to bring about our very demise. So that you, too, might be a fool to the cause.

We give of ourselves to serve a nation, to serve the greater good. Attempting all things and achieving what we can. But these achievements are tamped down and smothered by ill-defined borders, vague missions, opaque or non-existent end states, and loyalty to higher entities we will never know.

And the people that made you who you are, the people that you serve, all they want is one thing: for you to execute violence on their behalf, to sacrifice for them in the name of a country that you have been taught to love with your whole heart.

This is our reality, and you are in it right alongside me, saying your lines exactly as written, standing right where they tell you to stand. You were created to be a soldier, their soldier. And you have been their soldier since birth, whether you know it or not. From the moment you first felt the warmth of that light that illumines all men, calling you to true freedom, every endeavor, every task, every moment of your infancy, your youth, your education, your training was designed to pull you away, to extinguish that light and put you on the loop to worship a violent, soul-crushing system of manmade power and dominance. You were created for your own destruction, a professional soldier, giving your oath to the rulers of our day, yet still thinking you might be capable of being true to yourself, a compendium of internal issues and anxieties grounded in a division deep within your heart. It's this division they require in order for us to function in accordance with their will.

Because we know a soldier must wake up each day wanting nothing more than to kill an enemy, to be nothing more than a ground-pounding grunt: dirty, nasty, frontline, conventional soldier. Nothing more, nothing less. To fight and win. A blind berserker on the field of battle. And if you are not provided an enemy in each waking moment, by God, you will go out and find one. Even if it kills you. Even if it kills me. This is what makes a professional soldier in service to a grateful nation: the will to destroy that which is your enemy.

There are a few of you in here now, forced to attend a retirement ceremony that feels so distant to your own experience, so beyond your ability to understand, that already know this to be true. You're fools with a compunction to fight. You don't know why, you just know that you need to fight. You will, just as I have foolishly done, seek out fights for the rest of your life. Every game you've played, every book you have ever read, every endeavor you've ever embarked upon, has been a sad substitute, an illusion, a fiction to your created purpose. For we know nothing other than what we think we are, what we were made to be, the way we were created for service in a world made for someone else. And you must accept this as your truth or be done with it here and now. Because I will now tell you why you need to fight, why you are so angry with your enemy, why you must defend our nation as you have been instructed. You, my dear friends, are actually made for something else. And if you will just pause for a moment and reflect, this is a truth you have always known. Yet, in order to remain a soldier, you must remain a distant and aloof fool just as I was for so many years. So the question becomes: for whom do you wish to be a fool? You or them? Do you wish to be a fool for those around you, or those you call family and neighbors and friends? To be the worker, the farmer, the artist, the teacher, the craftsman, you were when you first saw the light, before they worked so assiduously to snuff out all that is holy within you, all that is your labor, your very existence, before they decided you would be a fool for them and them alone by making sure you were divided from everything you once loved and cherished?

For we the people are tragically flawed, with no more hope in running this organization than we have in exacting revenge against the system that created us. Stop looking for something else inside the beast. There is nothing else. Either become blissfully ignorant of this fact and accept your destiny or cast it off and walk away. This is how it must be.

What they need is for you to never give in to the burning shit and trash fires all around you, to set aside any acknowledgment of the futility in questioning the burn pit, the questioning of outpost placement, the curiosity about their borders, so that you might remain blissfully ignorant, as you must, waiting within yourself for that precious moment that will validate your existence, make you come alive, make you rise above the mediocrity of their civilization, the mediocrity of their power, if even for a brief moment, to say . . . *there's a kingdom I do not yet know, and it is inside of me. There can be nothing in this life more meaningful, more fulfilling, more awe-inspiring than the breathless realization that you are exactly what you say you are, undivided, undisrupted: complete and wholly human.*

So you are either a fool, as I have been all these years, or you must wake up to the reality of your existence. No pretense, no phoniness, no leadership philosophies, no building of organizational synergy. Whom do you serve? For whom will you be a fool?

You must decide.

I know the moment I stop rambling, the moment I close this speech, and the second I walk away from this podium, I am done. My work here finished. The one thing I know I was really good at I must now walk away from and try to reconcile these divisions made within me over so many years, divisions which I fear are much too wide to be joined. What was once real in me was slowly, methodically smothered inside notebooks, in family trips, in unfinished journals, on baseball fields and basketball courts, in woods and mountains and streams and cities and towns all across our nation, so that what tiny flicker of light was left could finally be fully extinguished on the field of battle.

So you're either a soldier or you're not a soldier. The choice is simple. The world is full enough of mediocrity, and bad ideas, and stupid rules and things that really don't matter once you've tasted what is truly real. It is only now that I recognize the limits of my own understanding.

I know I am rambling. I should have ended this long ago. The very idea of me wrapping this up right now, of stopping this little speech I've been given the opportunity to deliver, terrifies me. I have never before been scared of the present. But as we all know, so we have all been told, all good things must come to an end. Being a soldier is no exception . .

It was at this point that I would take a swig from my flask and again slowly survey the audience, adopting the same pensive and introspective glare I have mastered over many years of staring at sunsets through the blurry haze of a burn pit much too wide and not nearly deep enough to serve its intended purpose. I grab my Colt Peacemaker from the podium, place the barrel against my temple and pull the trigger, exiting the soldier's loop of my own accord, handing the torch of foolishness from old hands to new hands, in real time, a one-out/one-in policy singularly executed. I fall back, crumple to the ground, fold in half, my head slamming into the floor the same way my radioman's head dove into the dirt.

"Ha . . . Ha . . ."

A soldier's death. The death, dear reader, you wanted all along.

24.

IN THE CHOOSE-YOUR-OWN-ADVENTURE BOOK I started writing in the back of a tripartite notebook when I was in the sixth grade, the hero of the story pilots a spacecraft in which he is the lone occupant. He travels across the galaxy in search of a long-lost twin. The only memory the protagonist has of this twin is a vague recollection of being together side by side in space-age high chairs at a long, empty dinner table. The memory of this shared meal is a blur, the hero's twin remains a nameless, faceless unknown, ceaselessly banging a metal tray. The rest of the story, of how this character and his twin were nursed and fed together by a machine specifically designed to make them hate each other and of how they then came to be separated as part of an experiment in which men were pitted against one another in a grand scheme to spur competition among neighboring planets for the benefit of a few evil scientists, was told to the protagonist by a sympathetic tutor.

Options in the book always involved whether or not to fight an evil villain found on another planet or to leave the planet and continue the search for the long-lost twin. Taking the option to fight always led to a page near the end of the notebook and the death of the hero. At some point, had I continued the story, a fight would have had to commence in which the hero defeats the evil villain and is reunited with his twin. A choose-your-own-adventure book in which the reader is just led to jump around from page to page getting the main character killed would not have been very engaging.

The book, of course, like so many things in this transitory life, was never finished. And so here I am now, thinking about an unfinished childhood book while spending the last week with the poor soul charged with taking over my broken company of men. Our inventories have gone well. The usual switching around and covering for each other and laying the same items out two or three times in hopes the new guy will not notice takes place just as it always has, just as it ever will. At this point we all know there are only forty-seven compasses in the army's inventory. We just keep passing them around for each change of command.

At the end of a day of accounting for equipment and various briefings about the area of operations and the way ahead for the new guy, I spend my evenings either in the barn or locked away in my room. My replacement has opted to set up a cot in the main sleeping quarters, with the men. And I envy him for it.

The insurgents across the border are invigorated after our last fight, and as the incoming siren rings again for the third morning in a row, just a mere second before five rounds land inside the compound, I realize our nation's occupation of Combat Outpost Chemera is coming to a close. Someone echelons higher will suddenly come to the conclusion that this post no longer holds strategic value and that the local border police are well trained and prepared to assume the defense of the entire compound. There will be a small ceremony to which a smattering of military leaders from the army of the nation we have invaded will attend as well as a few local elders. Roughly half of the border police will put on their uniforms for the ceremony and then immediately go back to growing vegetables, tending their goats, hosting dinner and dance parties, and living their lives as if nothing ever happened here.

This last five-round salvo by the insurgency, a day before my chain-of-command ceremony, damaged a truck and destroyed the makeshift gym. A sergeant on his way to the gym was injured in the blast and had to be evacuated. He will recover.

We have completed all the required inventories and briefings required of us. My replacement, a competent officer and a good man, is resigned to leave me alone for the day as he makes the rounds and gets to know the company of paratroopers he is about to command. In less than twenty-four hours he will become responsible for everything that does and does not happen on Combat Outpost Chemera. And I want nothing but the best for him, and his command, and for the men I once led, for better or worse.

My room is all packed up, along with my gear, ready once again to be used as a storage closet for excess MREs, batteries, or duffel bags. I've hidden myself away in the barn for most of this final afternoon and evening of my command. And I wait.

The first sergeant peeks his head around the corner.

"You in here, sir?"

"I am, First Sergeant. What's up?"

"You good?"

"I am, First Sergeant. Very good indeed."

"Mind if I talk to you for a minute?"

I am not in the mood, yet I recognize that I owe this man, who has endured so much for our nation, at least some closure to my command and to our relationship, such as it is.

"What's up, First Sergeant?"

He steps into the shadows with me and pulls up an MRE box a few feet away.

"Sir, I just want to let you know that I'm here if you need anything. I know you and I haven't always seen eye to eye . . ."

I know where this is going and I need to steer the conversation elsewhere. The first sergeant and I have always enjoyed a distant, if not awkward, relationship of mutual respect for our individual lots in life. This is not a bad thing. We have each played our role as cogs in the machine for which we were individually created. He has done a good job in doing what I need him to do, of filling the role in the company he is supposed to fill. He has a job to do and he does it, never questioning the task at hand. But what I do not need right now is a pep talk. "Stop, First Sergeant. Thanks for trying, I guess. I appreciate it. I do. But can I ask you something?

"Of course."

"Now what?"

"What do you mean, sir?"

"What do I do now? What do I say when someone asks what happened? Because the way I see it, there are only two options for me now: feel guilty for the rest of my life for a sin I'm not entirely sure I committed, or spend the rest of my life pretending somebody owes me something: victimizer or victim."

"What sin are we talking about? Not finding Alastor? Losing a soldier?"

"Both, First Sergeant? Or neither? But it's not that simple, is it? Nothing ever is. The realty, the sad truth of the situation is even bleaker."

"How's that?"

"I am sentenced, just like all of us, you included, to spend the remainder of my life pretending all this mattered."

"Whoa, sir. It matters. You know it matters."

"Does it, though? Matters how?"

"It matters because we swore an oath. It matters because, because it just does, we know it does, we know—"

"We know nothing. You mean freedom and liberty and service? Duty, honor, country?"

"I'm not sure I get where you're coming from."

"Exactly, First Sergeant. Because you are the perfect soldier: loyal, disciplined, committed. I am none of those things. But you know how I actually feel right now?"

"Not really, but I'm getting curious."

"This is an untenable, unsustainable position. None of us asked for this. It just happened to us. Do you not see that?"

He stares back, empty to what I am saying, refusing to take my bait, a true company man to the core and a credit to our nation.

"How do I not see what, sir? That we don't get to choose what war we fight? That not everything in life will go our way? We volunteered. We have no beef anymore. I've heard you say it yourself. We are soldiers. We fight where we are told and we win where we fight."

"Well, I'm through fighting, First Sergeant. I'm through being their fool. I won't play this game anymore, one giant clusterfuck designed to make them feel good about themselves in each singular moment of a lifetime of increasingly dull moments."

"With all due respect, sir, I honestly have no idea what you're talking about."

"I was a soldier once, a happy fool for an idea, created for nothing more than to give our nation another product in which to pass the time, another event to placate the desperation of our history, until we are forgotten about and they move on to the next item on the agenda. But no more. I'm done."

I can see the confusion building up inside him settling at the surface waiting for me to go too far, to cross the line one dare not cross. But I no longer understand where these borders are and who established the margins to which I am somehow forever committed. I am trying to push him to the brink, the instinct to fight welling up within me:

"First Sergeant, this whole thing is a do-over. They fucked it up, destroyed everything, everyone, every place, and now it's up to us to rebuild our lives for ourselves, create a kingdom of our own in which we can sit back and bask in our true light, in all the things we were meant to be."

"Okay, sir. You want to know what I'm good at?"

"I already know. You're good at being a soldier. But we're all going down with this ship, and they don't care. For no other reason than an abstraction. For power and revenge that is not our own."

"Yeah, I don't know about this, sir. This is getting a little deeper than I want to go. But what I do know is something you have always said yourself: *men, we have a job to do.* And I agree with you 100 percent. I love when you say that. The men love when you say that. But we don't get to decide what that job is, do we? We just do it. I thought that's how you felt too."

I stare back at him, the awkwardness I have always felt between us now growing to a rift filled with anger. I want him to say something else, something that is not company-man drivel. But he will not. Not now, not ever. He is all that is good and pure and loyal in your country.

"You know, sir, with all due respect, you're no different than Private Alastor when you think like this. We did all this for him because he volunteered for something, and then didn't like what he volunteered for? Well, it doesn't work like that. Soldiers died for him. Soldiers lost their lives in the search for a traitor. Now how can *you* not see *that*! You can stare off into the sunset and read your books but you can't . . ."

"Yes. I can! Books I finally understand: we are lonely sailors being led by a loveless, hate-filled captain on a ship called revenge . . ."

I take a deep breath, regain my composure.

". . . and we have to abandon ship."

We sit for a moment in total silence, each weighing our next words and understanding that to articulate them, to keep going, would only lead to regret. He no longer takes me seriously, or at least he does not know what to make of me anymore. He stands up and looks down at me. I continue to stare at my mountains.

"I'm going to go check on stand-to. I assume you're headed back to your room, where you will continue to hide? Where you've hidden yourself for weeks now? You know, a lot of the men wanted to talk to you today, maybe even hoped you would give them one more big speech. Like old times. You at least owe them that. They love you, sir, for better or worse. And I know you love them, too."

"Good night, First Sergeant."

"This is wrong, sir. I don't know what happened, but you have to fix it. And I'm here for you if you need me. If you need to talk."

"Thank you, First Sergeant. You can go check on stand-to now."

He stands there for a moment, lost as to what to do, confused for the first time in his career.

"Good night, sir."

He remains in place, hoping I'll change something about the last moments of our conversation. But I will not. And he slips out of the barn and into the evening, returning to his sacred duty.

I knew that I would always be here to tell you my story. Each day, month, year, just another notch in the belt of time that says: *You live here now. You are forever . . . present.* This fight has been unfolding my entire life, each moment clashing with every thought, word, and deed. The truth, dear reader, is that I am not, nor have I ever been, the soldier you need me to be.

0355. My quarters are dark. The space feels empty, devoid of the pressures, the burden, of command, the last six hours spent in lonely anticipation. I gather my weapon and assault pack, a single magazine of ammo, and a few sundry items to sustain me. *Travel light, freeze at night.* I fold one single, clean uniform, name-tag facing up, and lay it at the end of my cot, placing my book about whaling, a book I now understand all too well, on top of the neat stack.

0400. No moon tonight, dark as the bottom of a rusty shit bucket, the occasional flicker of a red lens across the compound the only evidence that anyone is still alive at Combat Outpost Chemera. Shadows, dark hallucinations, forgotten silhouettes move in the guard towers as I make my way towards the front gate. Sad, tired soldiers go up the ladders. Sad, tired soldiers come down the ladders. Another shift change complete. The new shift, still half asleep, situates themselves for their hour-long turn at the post. The old shift walks back to their huts to get some sleep before they do it all again, this time under a new commander, hopefully a commander with no boundaries within himself with which he must wrestle.

It should be well known by this point that soldiers never check their night vision goggles at the beginning of shift. This is truth. Tired, complacent, easily resigned to fate, such is the demeanor of all soldiers. Soldiers wait till at least twenty minutes into their shift when the realization sets in that so little time has passed. Then and only then do they occupy themselves with the unnaturalness of night vision, a novelty that never goes away, while their partners nap.

I turn to survey my post for the last time, a post I was at one time charged with commanding. I am making a decision that will affect thousands of men as they scour and patrol the desert and mountains just as I scoured and patrolled the desert and mountains on a mission of *disruption.* I will bring shame and ridicule to my family and to my country, a family I will never know again, a country I will never see again, a country I once loved with all my heart.

I want to leave a note that says *don't look for me. I have left and I do not wish to be found.* Or I want to be able to explain to you that *yes, I believe Alastor is a tragic mistake that should not have happened. He never belonged here. He is not a soldier. He is a traitor that failed himself and failed us in the exact same way I have failed. I failed our nation. And I failed you, dear reader.*

But I know this will be pointless. I am unclear myself as to whether I believe these sentiments or I simply want to leave you a contrived message that will render me crazy, a bit emotionally touched, and might absolve me from guilt in my actions. Regardless, you are going to look for me. You will hunt me down in order to save me, offended by my every thought, word, and deed. You will expend millions of dollars and thousands of man-hours searching for me, somewhere, lost in a land foreign to you. Because we never leave a fallen comrade. So I am told. Yet I have fallen farther than any comrade ever could. My place lies just on the other side of those mountains, tucked away in a nearby valley. No past and no future, only the present. You may only wish to find me so that you may destroy me, take away my power to escape, the power still in me to walk away from you. But I am too far gone. Breathing freely for the first time since my youth I slip out the front gate and into the darkness, more alive than I ever felt in any firefight when the crack and whir of bullets zipping by my head was as real as the smell of the godforsaken burn pit stinging my nostrils even now. Wrapped in an all-encompassing silence, the ribs of the whale surround me. The absence of sound envelopes me.

I turn around and tape a note onto the metal gate, a page ripped directly from Alastor's journal, a note that represents the last vestige of a man's journal, his sacrosanct thoughts, his letters to a light he found buried deep within, speaking to his soul as all poetry must:

> It is a woe too deep for tears, when all
> Is reft at once, when some surpassing Spirit,
> Whose light adorned the world around it, leaves
> Those who remain behind, not sobs or groans,
> The passionate tumult of a clinging hope;
> But pale despair and cold tranquility,
> Nature's vast frame, the web of human things,
> Birth and the grave, that are not as they were.

Then I add my own addendum to his words at the bottom of the journal entry:

> 38 y.o., 648 AB, 211 H, 31 HR, 122 RBI, .326, NL Pennant
> 39 y.o., —Whereabouts Unknown

Hugging the outside walls of Chemera so as to not disturb sleeping guards, men who might see visions of past and future wars in their slumber, men who must be blissfully ignorant, caring only for those who have next guard shift and what time breakfast is served, the smell of the smoldering ashes of our civilization grows stronger with each liberating step.

I toss the remainder of Alastor's journal into the orange embers of a burn pit much too wide and not nearly deep enough to hide our daily collection of trash as a personal favor to the treasonous deserter, the completion of a task he did not know needed to be completed. The leather book lands with a dull thud and nestles deep into the smoldering embers as the electric cloud of ash kicked up by the diary stings my nostrils.

I have always known who you are, dear reader, and that you would need to be told of these events, by me, even when I am unable to fully understand who I am. But the story is told, such as it is, such as it ever will be. It is our truth to be held close to our heart. It is our light, nearly smothered, now newly alive, breathing the fresh air of a reborn life in the knowledge that I will do no more fighting, delighting to do no evil.

The story now complete, I ask that you forgive my transgressions, such as they are. For you may call me what you will. But you should know that war is not a place for brooders or the romantic, dreamers or poets, the sentimental or the naive. War is a place for soldiers, soldiers created in the image of strength and power, like men in vengeful pursuit of a mighty beast found in a book about whaling.

I make my way through the rocky foothills to a border between two countries, one at war with an insurgency and one pretending not to support that insurgency, and scramble to the mountaintop, to a boulder that saw one life lost in search of another. Among the footprints, empty shells, and bloodstained rocks of past battles, I wait. Two small birds scream and squawk overhead, disturbing the silence as the rays of the morning sun push against the walls of the white sky, creating a new day. Alastor crests the hill and approaches, his steps slow but sure, his eyes unwavering in hopeful gaze.

All has collapsed inside of me now. And the great beast rolls on, just as it always has, just as it always will.